THE REPENTERS

ACKNOWLEDGEMENTS

There are saints among us, found in the deepest fractures, serving without promise of award or apotheosis. Not willing to risk omitting any names, I would simply like to thank these selfless counsellors and educators – and all those who live to foster the futures of broken childhoods.

To get into the specifics now, I'd like to acknowledge my mother and father, Merle and Ashraff, who have supported me since my pre-teens through this mostly tricky and thankless undertaking of mine; Shivanee Ramlochan, my editor and friend, who has probably vivisected three iterations of this manuscript; Jeremy Poynting and Jacob Ross, both a pleasure to work with and both instrumental to the final draft, as well as the rest of the folks at Peepal Tree Press for giving this book a shot; and finally, Portia, who is there for me whenever I hit a dead end, or any of the various other occupational hazards that come with this literary calling.

KEVIN JARED HOSEIN

THE REPENTERS

PEEPAL TREE

First published in Great Britain in 2016
Peepal Tree Press Ltd
17 King's Avenue
Leeds LS6 1QS
England

ISBN13: 9781845233310

Supported using public funding by
ARTS COUNCIL
ENGLAND

'Those are the orders,' replied the lamplighter.
'I do not understand,' said the little prince.
'There is nothing to understand,' said the lamplighter.
'Orders are orders. Good morning.'
And he put out his lamp.

— *The Little Prince*, Antoine de Saint-Exupéry.

I

THE SAINTS

'This is a long road that has no turning.'

★

The people put me in St. Asteria after my mother and father was murdered. Nobody was ever too sure what really went down. All they know is that on that day, old Mrs. Boodram overhear some commotion from the house next door – glass breakin, cupboards rattlin, woman screamin out for the God Almighty, the works. After the old woman ring up the house and get no answer, she push poor Mr. Boodram to go over and check out the scene.

The old man, after trampling a path through the overturned kitchen, nearly shit his pants as he cross into the ransacked living room. Armoire lying face down, shards of pots strewn cross the floor, where the light filterin in from the window shining right on a little boy wading in a shallow pool of gore. Splashed on the floor, as if hurl from a pail.

The body and the blood.

The statement and testimony.

I being honest when I say I can't remember a damn thing.

I was only two. I ain't know how people expect me to remember.

They tell me that I coulda be repressing memories bout the day – that if you open up my brain, you'll find the sorrow swimmin in some knot of nerves in there. I joke round a couple times and say how the damn thing was probably my own doing. How it was probably me – my bloody-up two year old self – who mastermind the massacre. Nobody ever find that kinda joking round funny. I never bother to follow up on any of it. Never had no need to. The talks and therapy wasn't worth jack shit either. It ain't have no cut to heal if the knife never break the skin.

Have a saying: Time longer than twine.

Learn that and you can get through the day. In the end, it's okay. Even if you die, it's okay. It ain't God's business to save the bodies. People see the bright and the young go out in a muzzle-flash and get the wrong idea. Give God a chance with your soul and you will be okay. You have to open up and look at the grand scheme of things. All bad things come to an end, but not without casualties. God don't owe you anythin beyond that point. The ones who survive are the people who God have His eye on. And I could tell you one surefire thing. Since the clock start tickin, since before I could remember, God has watched over me.

My parents' names, they had tell me, was Ishmael and Myra Sant. Ishmael succumb to two cutlass wounds to the chest. Never seen it myself but I can't help but picture a big bloody crucifix tattooed to the flesh. Myra collect a knife to the jugular. Think there was rape involve too. I'm only sayin that because when Sister Mother and Father Anton took me to the sanctuary that day to tell me bout the whole damn mess, I know they was holdin back, just from their tone. The story don't seem messy enough. Some pieces was missin. For my own good. See, Father Anton ain't have it in him to mention rape to a child. Careful what you put in your mind, he always say, cause it's hard to get it back out.

The church always smell like wood shavings. There was always something heavy in there, a pressure slowly fillin the spaces. During choir and the Sunday sermons, I use to hear the bats squeakin between the roof and the rafters. I mention it once, and the others look at me like I was mad. Like I had bats in the belfry.

I was twelve then, give or take. Most of the others was round that age at the time.

Father Anton to my right and Sister Mother to my left. Father Anton had his hand sling over the back of the bench. Sister Mother sat upright as she always did, a squint-eyed gaze on the crucifix the whole time. I grab my knees and rock back and forth, my eyes focus on the glints of light shootin through the stained speckled window of Mother Mary, dappling the floor.

Father Anton mutter under his breath, 'All of that just for a little bit of money.'

'The wicked stop at nothing. Don't underestimate them,' Sister Mother say straight out. She turn and say, 'Jordon, are you listening to me, boy?'

'Yes, ma'am,' I reply, my voice quick and faint.

Hushed, but unapologetic, she say, 'You owe your life to God. Forgetting a debt doesn't mean it is paid. I'm here to remind you, boy, if you don't honour what was done for you, and you end up lying with the dogs, you're well on your way to rise with the fleas.'

Sister Mother was an old white woman, come to Trinidad from God-knows-where. She was the boss. She wasn't Old Testament, but when she enter rooms, she coulda rasp the chatter right outta the air. We'd all snap to attention quick-quick. Her face was hard – skin stretching tight over bone at her sallow cheeks. Grey eyes like samurai steel, tipped with piercing right-eous pupils. Her hair, if she had any, was always concealed by the wimple and veil. She was tall. A woman with height like that, you would picture to be hunchback, but she always make it her business to keep her back stiff and sit up straight. She make it our business too – all of her children at St. Asteria had to follow suit. Her children also included her superfluity of nuns – that's the collective noun for nuns, yes, a *superfluity*. Learn that I did.

She never pretend to come from Trinidad, or the twentieth century. Never try to rinse her accent with patois or Creole. Sometimes she seem to go outta her way to be as otherworldly as possible. More than once, she declare that the only people who excel in this country is the ones who reject it, meanin the ones who coulda swim outta the black hole that is *sweet, sweet T and T*. After all, most people who excel here – in the ways that matter – make the move of clearing their throat of the acidic, sulphurous phlegm that is the Caribbean dialect.

Aye – her words, not mine.

During dinnertime, Sister Mother use to put on some old-timey folksy music on this ancient record player she had. The music was for her and her alone – you didn't have to like it, but you could *not* challenge it. Doing that was like Oliver Twist asking Mr. Bumble for more gruel. Tell you, she was the boss. The songs was in English, but in one of them funny foreign accents. French. Or Scottish. Or German. Shit, I ain't know. Never coulda tell the blasted difference. Not sure if the others did either. We was too busy trying to sit up straight and chew seven times before swallowin. We use to count it, because she use to be countin it too.

'Sometimes I feel it is hopeless,' Father Anton say, suckin on his gum. 'I try to teach them to be good. But they're still going out in a world that is not.'

She say to him, 'We aren't preparing them for this world, Father. We prepare them for the one after.'

Looking at me, she say, 'Those men who killed your parents took away everything your family could have been in this life – they were evil. But they saw the Lord in you. The fear of God struck them and they couldn't touch you.'

Father Anton was still mumblin, 'Just for a lil bit of money. All this nonsense – '

Sister Mother clear her throat. 'You're still alive. You're still in control of your fate – *you* are the captain of your soul. Am I making myself clear? You didn't choose to come here to St. Asteria. But you can choose where to go from here. Don't be fooled. The mills of God grind slowly but they grind finely. This is a long road that has no turning…'

'How you feeling, Jordon?' Father Anton cut in. 'You upset?'

I say, 'No. Not upset, no.' And I really wasn't, but I don't think I coulda ever convince the old man otherwise. Something in my tone maybe. The whole time I know him, he never seem like he age a day. The man drifted outside time. He was a mountain – tallest man I ever come across. You'd never see him without his cassock. Working for God was a full-time job, he say, and one must always wear the uniform on the job. His dark skin lost some considerable amount of its hue as the years went by, as if it was washed out by worry, as if his skin turn to shale. He had the whitest hair and beard, like chalkdust smeared on ashes. His glasses obscured his wall-eyed gaze and the bags under his eyes.

Father Anton held a picture of Ishmael and Myra between his thumb and forefinger. He flick it like it was a playing card. Was from a cutout of a newspaper. A photo with the caption, *HAPPIER TIMES: Ishmael and Myra Sant on their wedding day.* They pose side by side at the steps of a small rural church. He in his cheap tuxedo, she in her hand-me-down dress. He had short hair, and she had long pincurls. He had squinty eyes, and she had big eyes. He was tall, and she was small. He was Indian and she was African. Even though they was such opposites, they had the same broad smile.

They look like nice people. That was all I coulda say.

Father Anton thought something woulda turn on, some switch woulda click, some hundred-watt bulb woulda blaze a path through my dark memories. But nothing ever come. Not no spiritual shudder, not no tightenin of the asshole. The earth didn't contract and squeeze a reaction outta me. My nose turn up a little, my mouth twistin slack as I shake my head at him. I just couldn't look at the picture and feel what the old man wanted me to feel. For a second, it was as if I coulda see into my own mannequin stare. Like I was outside myself.

Father Anton lean in towards me, cradling his chin in his palm. 'How come you asked about them?'

That was the deal for some of us at St. Asteria. If you wanted to know the disastrous shambles of the past, St. Asteria waited until you asked. It was a rite of passage, almost. But I didn't care bout knowin. Rey did. So I tell them the truth.

Sister Mother furrow her brow. 'You mean *you* didn't want to know?'

'I don't really think bout it. I here now. That's enough for me.'

She shake her head and Father Anton scratch his neck, both of them in disapproving silence. Then they both put their heads down. They each held my hand – Father Anton, my right and Sister Mother, my left. And the three of us pray to God. But my eyes stray up to the crucifix over the altar. Its slanted grimace. Its blank wooden eyes. I know the only people who say, 'God is good' is the ones who God is good to, or those wishing that God *was* good to them. At that time, reflecting on the images they put in my mind – the overturned room, the toddler in the blood, and the light shining over him – it was them three words that loop in my head: God is good.

When I went back to my room to tell Rey the details, he was quiet at first. And then he ask, 'How you feel when they tell you?'

I just give him a shrug. 'Normal.'

Rey was already shack up here at St. Asteria when I'd first come through these doors. And we live together in the same room since that. He was the shortest boy in St. Asteria. The big head and big glasses didn't help the image either. He was always tryin to grow a 'fro, but Sister Mother use to strap him to the toilet and shave it off.

St. Asteria ain't like the other homes – ain't pack like them, anyway. Was just eight of us or so at the time. I remember when we had to lay mattresses on the floor. That was all we had till Sister Mother manage to scour a donation from the Government – election time is always good for things like that, and she was savvy enough to always take advantage of it. I remember the people put up an article in the papers and all when that grant come through. Best thing we buy was a bunk bed for each room, though the first fights we had with each other in St. Asteria was base round deciding who was gon get the top bunk. Rey and me just decide to switch top and bottom every other week. Never had no worries with Rey. Never had no fight, no beef, no squabble. Not at the time, anyway.

We was never too close, not like how you woulda expect children of misfortune to be. You'd think grief would be a bond between people, cause it's all they know. Rey was in the same boat as me, too young to properly digest and absorb tragedy into the blood. I think we both use to think somethin was wrong with us because we couldn't feel nothin. Possibly hit him harder than it hit me. I think we had more in common than he woulda ever let on, but he thought I was strange, and he didn't want to be like that, so he disguised our similarities. He always feel the need to reassure everybody that he was just like them, even though nobody here was like anybody else.

How Rey end up here – his father use to beat his mother. Was just to keep the woman in check, never to kill. But drunk, the line between manners and murder tend to blur. So, the inevitable happen. When he realize what happen, the man went out back and grab the bottle of Gramoxone. He sit in the tool shed, take one sip – two sips, and then quench his dying thirst. The only thing Rey remember, and vaguely, was the man bawlin out for him. Rey couldn't remember nothin the man say, just the gargle of ruptur-ing vocal cords as the man try to utter his last words, whatever they was.

Average Trini homicide-suicide.

And just the same, Father Anton take Rey to the sanctuary and show him a photo of his parents. I imagine he has a whole deck of them somewhere in a drawer. I always wonder whose past is held in the aces, and whose is trapped in the jokers. Rey's reaction wasn't no different from mine. He just watch the picture, shake his head and pray for deliverance like Father tell him to. Didn't matter. Didn't know who them people was. Didn't care to know.

He only ask because Rico woulda tease him bout it and tell him how he hear his father was a drunkard and a wife-beater. Was a true story, but Rey was tired of Rico knowin more than he did. Rico use to know everybody's business in St. Asteria, and was always confident in the facts he coulda produce bout people's lives. How he coulda access the files and know what was in the cards we was dealt was one of the most troubling mysteries.

Rey nudge me with his shoulder and spill the big news, 'I hear we gettin a new nun end of the week.'

'Where you hear that?'

'Just the talk I hearin from Rico and them.'

'Well, you know Rico know everything.' I lowered my voice. 'Boy, I hope she replacing Bulldog.'

In a gurgle of laughter, he say, 'You wish. Ain't hear bout she replacin nobody. But hear this. I hear she fresh.'

'Fresh?'

'Young.'

'Young, how? Everybody old here, boy. Them does say Sister Kitty young and she pushin forty.'

'No, boy. I hear this one now come outta school. And real pretty. Them boys sayin she lookin straight outta one of them Indian movie.'

I raise my eyebrows. 'So, what day she comin?'

He shrug. 'I dunno. But Kitty ain't really take to she, I hear.'

'Why?'

'Not sure. That's just what Rico say.' He chuckle. 'Guess what them fellas callin she already?'

He say it slow, restraining a giggle, 'Sister Mouse.'

And so the trio was complete – we had a Bulldog, a Kitty and a Mouse.

When the next week come round, Sister Mother summon us to the living room. Both the boys and the girls. See, the structure of St. Asteria, the boys live in the right wing and the girls in the left. The upstairs was for the nuns. Father Anton live right in his rectory, at the parish. Never had a night that the nuns was sleepin in any other place than upstairs. They had to live there. No child was allowed to go upstairs unless a nun was with them.

That ain't stop Rico and Quenton, though.

Them raggamuffins use to go up there all the time. Funny thing was that it didn't have shit up there. They use to go just because it was against the rules. Rico and Quenton was the two oldest boys in St. Asteria, like fourteen round the time I talkin bout here. They was together in another home before they come to St. Asteria. Was like an asteroid hit Earth the day they come. Sister Mother wasn't lyin when she say that they suffer a double dose of original sin. The first morning, they come strollin through the halls rapping the lyrics to *Pum Pum Conqueror*, alternatin.

Rico goin, *Pum pum fat, pum pum slim.*

And Quenton pickin up, *Pum pum bushy and pum pum trim.*

Quenton never took off his camo NY cap, because he didn't want people seein the bald spot above his ear. Rico the redman, claimed he fight and fuck his way outta two other homes before his ass get ship here.

It was because of them two that Sister Mother make the call to bring in another sister, though it take two months to receive a reply to the SOS.

When the junior nun show up the next week, she work up a sweat lugging a fat, old suitcase into the living room, the old leather cracked and peelin from the sides.

I hear Rico whisper to Quenton, 'Like she have a dildo collection in there, or what?'

Sister Kitty bite her lip and hold back a laugh. Wasn't sure if it was because of the lewd joke, or if she was just amused watchin the newcomer struggle. Sister Kitty was twine-thin, waist tapering under her habit, skin as pale as the moon. Her eyebrows inclined upward, her lashes thick like beetle legs. She had a bright megawatt smile. In this hot weather, her kohl-black hair stuck to her flushed cheeks, as if patted with a wet palm. For a woman pushin forty, I admit she was quite easy on the eyes – like a pretty lady posing as a nun, rather than a real one. A real NILF, as Rico put it – *Nun I'd Like to Fuck.*

A title now under threat. Two attractive nuns? Shit, was this a prank or a miracle?

Sister Mother make sure all of us clean up good for the day of the arrival. She douse us with perfume and tie white ribbons in the girls' hair, not a strand outta place. Spit-polished shoes and white socks pull right up, stretched taut. Yet she keep remindin us that good looks couldn't trump good manners.

She was standing beside the nun, hands clasped like a vice before her stomach. Was a funny sight. The junior nun was a smurf next to Sister Mother. I ain't think she woulda be that small.

She looked younger than I picture. Look like she coulda been twenty, if even that. Tiny slits in her cheeks appeared when she smile at us. When she laugh, she scrunched up her bob nose. She had a widow's peak. That was all I coulda see of her hair. The rest was cover up under the veil. Mostly, when I think bout Mouse on that day, though, I remember her as feathery – like she coulda just drift off with a breeze.

Sister Mother say, turning her chin up to us, 'Children, this is our new addition to the St. Asteria family. Her name is Sister Maya Madeleine Romany. She was born right here in Trinidad. She enjoys reading the classics, so hopefully some of that can rub off on you. The Lord has brought her to us and we are very grateful to have her here.'

We stood side by side – boys on one side, girls on the next – and we recited in unison, 'The St. Asteria family welcomes you, Sister Maya.'

She put her hands together and bow her head. She was so enthusiastic, she was blushin. For some reason, I expect her to do a small curtsy. She looked like the type to do them things. She replied, 'Look at you all, just like little saints. I feel blessed.'

'You too young to be a nun!' Ti-Marie shoot out straight away, prompting a swell of stifled chuckles. Even I myself break into a grin. After dolling Ti-Marie up, getting her to wear a dress and gettin each bantu knot in place, we knew somethin was missing – a long stretch of scotch-tape for her big mouth.

As the junior nun part her lips to respond, Sister Mother whip a quick hand up with a sharp shush. The silence was immediate.

We wasn't sure if she was shushing her or Ti-Marie. She then whisper something in her ear. I coulda imagine her tellin her the same thing she tell me: *This is a long road that has no turning.*

'Jerrick! Jordon!' Sister Mother call out. 'Help Sister Maya with her belongings!'

Rico insist on carrying it by himself. He pull the suitcase up by the grip, draggin it up the stairs, the edge of it clattering against each step, much to the junior nun's dismay. She was flinching and mouthing, *Careful, careful,* but the words couldn't come out.

'*Jerrick!*' Sister Mother finally hiss. 'Watch your step! Jordon, help the boy! The back must slave to feed the belly!'

I didn't think I woulda find myself cooperating with Rico after he nearly break my finger a few days back. You know that dumb-ass game where someone would bend your finger back to your wrist till you scream *Mercy*! Well, as it happen, I was screamin out, 'Mercy! Mercy!' and Rico just keep bending my pinky back until it damn near break right off the joint. Never had no apology. Never ask for none. Play stupid games, win stupid prizes.

We both lift from the ends and haul it up together to her room. Rico take the suitcase and flop it on the bed, and she cringe as it hit the mattress. The room was small and she didn't look too pleased. The paint was flakin off the wall. Didn't have no window. We try to fix it up – our mission for the prior two days. Sister Mother assign the directives.

So we scrub and mop that floor, boy. We peel grime from brick. Take the broom to every cobweb and whap the corners till plumes of dust puff up against the walls. We wipe the dresser and shelves till not a speck was in sight – shoulda see them before, powder-up like they was seal away for centuries. Like relics in a tomb, a boneyard. You shoulda see the whole room before, dense and pulsin with grime. Swear it was alive, a throbbing hovel for spiders and lizards.

'Don't beat your small wee-wee too much over she, eh,' Rico whisper to me, though he was the one lickin her with his eyes.

I look at him from the corner of my eye. He nudge me, whispering again, 'She look like she could *get it*, though, eh?'

I ain't say nothin. Don't expect me to have no response to rubbish like that.

'You think anybody ever take she before?' His eyes dart back to her, one side of his mouth curlin up. 'I feel she never even see one before, boy. Or probably she fraid it. What you think?'

I narrow my eyes at him.

'Boys.' Her voice made us recoil.

Rico tip his chin at me and say, '*That* one there is the boy. I ain't no boy.'

'Gentlemen,' she say, smiling. Then she ask Rico, 'What's your name again, young man? Jerrick, right?'

'Yes, ma'am,' he say, grinnin. 'But you could call me Rico.'

She just raise her eyebrows at him. Then she direct her eyes at me. 'And what about you?'

I remember how my throat went dry at that moment. Tryin to talk but strugglin to lift my tongue. For a few seconds, I couldn't breathe. I was bunch up in a knot, frozen. I close my eyes – had to count to three. Only then the name coulda trickle out from the ice. 'J… Jordon Sant, ma'am.'

Rico let out a snort. The boy was stupid and smart at the same time. He had already sum up my adoration – my *veneration* of the new addition to St. Asteria. Probably know it before I did. He was good at sniffin out things like that – piling them together in his arsenal to use against you in the future. If you adore something and you let people find out, you expose a little bit of flesh to the world. Yes, affection is like a wound. Risk of infection come with it.

She smile at me. 'What do you say – want to help me unpack, Jordon?'

'All right.' My response come out in a polite breath.

Turning to Rico, she say, 'Well, that'll be all, Jerrick.'

He wasn't laughin no more. He was standin there, eyes sunken in his skull. 'You don't want me to help too?' He seem genuinely heartbroken. Didn't think to wonder why at the time. Perhaps Rico was feelin what I was feelin, but he was better at hidin it. Open his skin for the junior nun, probably.

'No,' she tell him straight. 'I'm sure the two of us could manage here. No need to burden yourself.'

'Burden? Is not a –'

'That's an order,' she say, stern.

'Yes, ma'am.' Rico's tone was sombre, workin hard to slide up the clutch in his throat. He leave the room and stamp step to step down the stairs. After she undid the suitcase latch, she dab a handkerchief on her forehead. She look at me with a nervous smile and say, 'What was I thinking, packing all this junk, huh?'

She flip the top open and I couldn't help but peek. Was mostly books and ceramic figurines. Never really care for books before, but I faked excitement over them. 'Wow, that's plenty to read.'

'You recognize anything?' she ask.

I shook my head. She was asking the wrong child. Poor Father Anton try to encourage everybody to read, but we ain't never bother. I think he use to feel bad, seeing the study with all them stacks of unread and half-read books – most of them donations, a few of them from his own personal library. All lain to waste.

She stack them into two neat piles on the bed. 'What's the last thing you read?' she ask me, still eyeing the books.

I shook my head again. 'I don't really read.' Guilty as charged. Never felt so bad bout not reading before. Not even when Father Anton and Sister Mother harass me daily that I wasn't expanding my vocabulary enough. Not when my teacher call me out on not knowin the difference between an adjective and adverb.

Her face went serious all of a sudden. A slight pallor in her lips, with apologetic slowness, she ask me my age.

So I tell her, tracing my toes on the floor, bracing for impact. She bite her bottom lip. 'Twelve years and not reading?'

'I just read the Bible sometimes.'

She paused and let out a small sigh. I know the sound of relief when I hear it. *Every*body, every soul that cross St. Asteria, always assume the worst when they see us. They assume none of us could even read, so they never want to ask direct, as if asking is accusin of some kinda sin. As if not knowin how to read is a kinda affront to mankind. At St. Asteria, I guess it was a sin, because all of us had not only had to read, but *enunciate* the Word of God.

I tell her, 'Never bother with much else. I never see the real purpose in readin somethin somebody just make up.' It wasn't a way to demean her passion. It wasn't even the truth. It was bait –

for her attention. And as she furrow her brow and run her finger down the bookspines, I know she was gon bite.

'They told me there's a library here.'

'The study – yeah.'

I led her down to the study. Really, it was just a few bookshelves, two old couches and a wobbly table. Thick walls, no windows, one door. I sat on the couch while Mouse browse the shelves. Piece by piece, she pile some books, make a stack out of them on the table: *Gulliver's Travels, Adventures of Huckleberry Finn, Oliver Twist, The Time Machine*. She ask me, 'You read these?'

I shrug. 'Hear bout them, but never bother.'

'You wanna start with these?'

'You mean, read them?'

'Mm-hmm.'

Oh God, was my first thought. It show, I'm sure, because she then say, 'Maybe I could lend you one of mine.' It seem that she was even a little desperate to make a connection. When you enter a dark room, you make sure you ain't alone, right?

'Yours?' I rub my thumbs together.

'From my suitcase.' She beckon me to follow her.

When we went back to her room, she sift through the books and produced the thinnest one. *The Little Prince*. The cover had a boy in pajamas standing on a small planet in outer space, but it didn't look like a space adventure. As she hand it to me, she say, 'You'll like this one, Jordon… There's one condition.'

'What?'

'That book is special to me, so keep it very, very safe. Can I trust you?'

You know, that was something. Not that nobody ain't ever trust me before. But nobody never trust me with something dear to them. She wasn't just testing me – she was testing herself. 'No dog-ears in it, I promise,' I say, giving her a nod. I held the book against my chest.

'Oh my, dog-ears? Well, if you do that, I don't think we could be friends for long.'

Then I help her organize her books on the shelf. I also laid the ceramics on the dresser. Was mostly swans, egrets, ducks. But mostly swans. Some of the other figurines was crafted out of shells. Had all kinda fancy shells. She named them for me – scallops, mussels, whelks, cockles, limpets, angel wings. They was painted and glued together to form frogs, rabbits, cats, all kinda animals.

'You make these?' I ask her.

A glint flashed in her eyes. 'My dad's a pilot, so he's been all over the world. Whenever he goes to a new country, if there's a beach, he's there. He collects rocks and shells. He doesn't like to buy them – I think he'd read once that the bigger, fancier shells weren't collected from the beach. They were taken from animals still alive. He just likes having them.'

'Still alive? These was living?'

She laughed. 'Shells are these creatures' armour, you know. Think about it. That's what my father told me. He said that we all have our own armour, one way or the other. Do you believe that?'

'I don't know.'

She shrug. 'Well, there were baskets upon baskets of shells at home. One day I got the idea to make animals out of them. This frog here,' and she held up a frog that was perched atop a mussel and had a scallop shell for a mouth, 'is from five different countries. You can imagine that? You're holding different parts of the world in your hand. The grand world in this little frog.'

She let me hold it. As I examined it, I said, 'I never really hold one before.'

'A frog?'

'A shell. Never went to the beach before.'

'The beach? What!' she blurt out. 'But this is Trinidad! Every-body's gone –.' Then she stop herself. She purse her lips and click her tongue. I never liked when people stop themself from sayin things round me, as if a sentence or a word could do me wrong. Make me feel like somethin was wrong with me.

We finish lay the figurines on the shelf. As I was bout to leave, I turned to her. She was still, her shoulders suddenly heavy, slumped, staring at the neat row of shell animals. The weight of the world suddenly bear down on her.

As I closed the door behind me, a feeling hit me. Ever since I was at St. Asteria, the door to this room was always locked, sealed off. I used to wonder what was behind it. I was living in this building almost my whole life and I hadn't even seen the whole place – because of this one mystery room.

When we was small, we had nicknames for all the nooks and crannies at St. Asteria, every peculiarity in the landscape. There was a park with a gazebo across the street. We call the gazebo Castle Grayskull, you know, from He-Man. The sprawling almond trees that patched the grass with shadows was the Evergreen Forest. The sharp dip in the ground near the parish was the Grand Canyon. When the rain fall, the drains woulda overflow into a shallow, circular concrete catchment at the corner of the entrance and fill it with tadpoles and guabines – that was the Fishing Pond. This mystery room, we use to call it the Sealed Cave. Now that it was occupied and I knew what was there, I couldn't help but feel some sense of completeness.

-2-
'Time runnin out. So we just havin we fun.'

★

We used to just call them the Sunday people – the thirty or forty heads that comprised Father Anton's flock. We play a big role. Together, we comprised the St. Asteria Children's Chorus. Was the one thing we coulda all come together for without cuss or quarrel. Father Anton admit to us once that he was sure that most of the Sunday people come for the blend of our voices, not for his sermons. I ain't sure how much truth it have in that. I mean, how many times people coulda stomach 'Enter into Jerusalem' and 'Nearer My God to Thee', really?

Sister Mother used to have us primped and propped up there in the chancel, fumigated with cologne and cast under the aura of the stained-glass Virgin Mary. I didn't have to think too hard bout how the Sunday people imagine us. Children of God. Evidence of His mercy. A reason to continue praying, a dose of blessed assurance. Sometimes, though, it feel like we was nothin but a feel-good, inspirational diorama. Up there, looking down at the flock, you always coulda feel some invisible barrier between yourself and the outside world, like there was a sheet of glass separatin the chancel from the nave.

The Sunday people never really come up to us. They probably thought the less they know bout the cracks in the glass, the better. I ain't blame them for thinkin that way – what was they gon say to a ragtag group like this? They ruffled our hair, patted our shoulders and we smiled on cue, and that was that.

Our asses depended on these Sunday people. Every dollar in the offering was part of the weekly paycheck. St. Asteria always banked on it, so we literally had to sing for our suppers. We had to train till our throats buss! Every Saturday afternoon, Sister Kitty would gather us to rehearse. We'd line up, girls in the front, boys in the back, one arm's length away from each other, Sister Kitty on a stool in front of us, strummin her wax-polished guitar.

If it's one thing I can say bout Kitty, she was good at making every child feel like they belong in that damn choir. She had a fancy name for everybody. Sookie was a coloratura, Jeannine was contralto, Ti-Marie was lyric soprano, Rey was a countertenor, Rico was a bass-baritone, Quenton and Elroy was baritones. Me, I was *evirato*. Nobody know what any of the damn words mean. It was white people words. Really, she coulda call we anything, but it make everybody feel like they had a place – that without their voice, the structure would fall apart.

When Kitty was twenty, during the short time she live and starve in New York, she manage to get cast in a musical called *Cats*, as a feline named Jennyanydots. Was her only notable theatre performance, so she never let you forget it. She probably like to think that the name, Sister Kitty, originated from this, and not because her real name was Katherine. She'd always remind us, 'Understand how privileged you all are to be under the tutelage of a Broadway thespian!'

Some of us thought the story was made-up. But then we realize it didn't really matter. She was a damn good singer – coulda rip all them tunes in true Disney princess style. I'd observe her while she was deep in song, eyes closed, lost in some shimmerin spotlight, back up on stage. Jennyanydots again. Cause when she was done, she'd open her eyes and I coulda see the muddy colours of reality smack her right in the face. Whatever dream she'd had, it continued without her – in another life, in another time. Part of her brain abandoned in a bell jar somewhere in Broadway, still pulsin from the music. Reality ain't somethin to be trifled with. It gon stab your ass if you ain't watch out.

Kitty had to be all she could be right here in old, ragadang Trinidad. The choir was everything to her. It was *hers*. But when you claim possession of somethin that don't belong to you alone, that's how trouble starts. Shit, that's how wars start. So when Sister Mother encourage Mouse to accompany Kitty for the next session, she send her into enemy territory. Kitty didn't say anythin in protest, but you didn't have to get past her flickering eyes to know she took it as nothin short of blasphemy.

We get through smooth with 'The Old Rugged Cross', 'Shine Jesus Shine' and 'Blessed Assurance'. But as soon as we hit 'Immaculate Mary', the friction began. That one had a tendency to do that. Nobody woulda ever think a short hymn coulda root up so much fuss. Ti-Marie and Jeannine would sing the verses and the rest of us would follow with the *Ave Maria* refrain in unison. But Ti-Marie woulda always try to outdo Jeannine – wouldn't be fair to say *try*, she used to plain-as-day outshine the girl. She had the swagger to go with the rhythm.

But instead of tellin Jeannine to raise her voice and match Ti-Marie's, Kitty would tell Ti-Marie to take it down a notch. She wasn't usually too harsh bout it, but that day, when Ti-Marie wouldn't obey, Kitty snap at her, 'Cut it out! Don't you already get enough attention?'

Church went quiet at that point. That is till Mouse call out, 'Let the girl sing!' She was sittin on the front pew, jiggling her feet to the music.

Kitty take a moment to breathe. 'She's a distraction.'

'Come on, don't be a hater!' Mouse threw in, and the room went dead quiet again. A queasy discomfort, lurchin soundlessly through the air. All eyes shot to Sister Kitty. I swear the woman was gon pop a vein. She was eyeing Mouse so hard that I thought that lasers was gon shoot out.

'I'm not being a *hater*,' Kitty said between breaths. 'Ti-Marie needs to learn that she's not the only singer in the room.'

'Don't stifle her. The girl's got talent.'

Did Mouse know what she was doing? She needed to get with the programme before hell break loose. Kitty was judge and jury when it come to how things sounded in this choir.

But Kitty was suddenly calm. 'Go ahead, Ti-Marie,' she said. 'Prove the haters wrong.'

Ti-Marie stood still – deer in the headlights, fiddling with her hands, nostrils flared in confusion. Kitty glared at the girl, waving a curled forefinger at her, 'Finish the song.'

We looked at each other and then at Kitty, drops of sweat beading under her nose. She put her palm to her forehead and give Ti-Marie a nod. Ti-Marie struggled through the hymn, each word crawlin out like blood from a cut. When it was done,

26

everyone was quiet for a while. Mouse, however, erupt in applause.

Ti-Marie's mouth curled into a grin. The girl was beaming. The iron gloom of Kitty's expression command the rest of us to silence. Mouse continued, 'If you keep this up, I wouldn't be surprised if you go into Broadway like your teacher!'

Well, that just put stars in Ti-Marie's eyes. None of us was accustom to compliments like that. Compliments was so rare that we used pocket them in our mind for the rainy days. What Mouse was doin was a dangerous thing. You could end up buildin a whole other world from the smallest of compliments only to watch people tear it down the next day. St. Asteria wanted us happy, but not too happy. Despair stem from bein too happy once upon a time.

'Broadway? For real?' She then turn to the rest of us, still grinning. 'You all hear that? Hollywood! Mm-hmm!'

Rico reply, shaking his head, 'Hollywood and Broadway is two different things, dummy.'

'That's not nice, Jerrick,' Mouse cut in. 'What do you want to be when you grow up, huh?'

'Growin up gon take a *long* time for Rico, Sister M,' Quenton said.

Rico laughed, punching Quenton's shoulder. 'Nobody ain't ask a question like that round here in a long-ass time, eh, boy?'

Mouse said, 'You must think about it. It's an important question.' She then turned to the rest of us. 'Sookie?' she asked. 'Have you ever thought about it?'

Sookie was our resident Caucasian, probably the only white orphan in this whole island. You couldn't bring up that she was the favourite, even though it was clear as day. Wasn't just her long straight hair or pretty face. Anytime she smiled or laughed, she brighten up the room. Sookie just had a way of breakin that covenant between bad luck and self-pity. Rico probably had the best way of describing her – Sookie was a hamster lost down in the sewer. 'I don't know,' Sookie said bashfully, playin with her hair. 'Ballerina?'

'That's awesome!' Mouse said.

'Sookie, you could dance?' Rey ask.

Sookie shook her head and we all laughed.

Mouse continued, 'What about you, Rey?'

'Astronaut!' he shot out.

'They have a helmet that could fit a head so big?' Rico asked.

Quenton high-fived him and added, 'He ain't need to go outta space. The boy head already big like a planet.'

'There's no need for that, gentlemen,' Mouse said. Sister Kitty still wasn't sayin a word, though she didn't look so angry no more. In fact, I swear she was fightin to hold back a smile.

'No need for what?' Rico shot back. 'You really think *anybody* here goin to become any of them things? Have a reason nobody here talk bout the future, Sister M. We know we have none.'

Mouse scrunched her brow. 'What are you talking about? We're going to ensure that all of you have a place in the world. There's no need – '

Rico cut in, 'Why you lyin? Everyone here know damn well nobody here gon be no astronaut. You really think Ti-Marie good enough for them white people to listen to? Educate yourself, Sister. No matter who Ti-Marie know or who she blow, the only way she ever gon be up on stage is if she moppin it.'

'Who put these thoughts into your head, Jerrick?' Mouse was tryin hard to steady her breathing. The desperation in her voice make me wonder if she found truth in his words and didn't want to hear it. Didn't want us to hear it. I could tell that the floodgates was bout to come apart. She turn to Kitty as if to say, *Help me out, Sister*, but Kitty just twist her mouth at her.

Rico hissed, 'You come here fulla shit.'

'That's not nice, Rico,' Ti-Marie cut in, standin akimbo.

'Nice ain't gon get you far, dummy.'

I open my mouth, but didn't say nothin at first. Then finally, a mutter escape, 'Rico, stop it.'

'What bout her?' Rico said, pointing at Mouse. 'You think she always wanted to be a nun?'

Mouse batted her eyes and a single tear dangled from her lash. I ain't never seen a nun cry before. I wasn't even sure if they was allowed to. I ball my fists up and scraped my knuckles against my pants. I didn't know how angry I was until I feel my tongue between my teeth. I imagine it's the same feelin people get when someone insult their mothers. Sister Kitty was just lookin on, lettin it happen, lettin Rico self-destruct. As if these things was supposed to happen – like God didn't want it to happen no different.

'Tell me, Sister M,' Rico keep on. 'When you was we age, you wanted to come to a shit-hole like this?'

Even Quenton realize Rico was goin too far. He nudge Rico's shoulder and whisper, 'Stop being an asshole, man. Control yourself.'

'*I'm* the asshole?' Rico throw his arms up in protest. 'I just tellin you like it is! Me, I'm not the asshole.' He pointed at Mouse and hissed, '*She's* the ass – '

That was when I swing at him. I miss so spectacularly that I make a complete revolution, dizzy myself and fall down flat. Everybody was too tense to even crack a gasp. They gather round me, their astonished faces formin a halo above me, through which I could see the crucifix and Jesus' cocked head takin pity on my hasty self.

Kitty finally turn to us, and then to Mouse. She shook her head and say to her, 'You can leave. I can handle them.' Then to the rest of us, 'Everyone, back in positions!' We shuffle back into place. Ti-Marie helped me up. She smiled at me and dusted me off. For a moment, I swear she lean over as if to kiss me before backin away at the last moment.

Sister Kitty put on a smile and announced, '"Immaculate Mary" once again from the top! One, two, three!'

As we began the refrain, Mouse walked away, a slight limp in her step. She wasn't battered, though. No, simply whiplashed.

After the rehearsal, I saw Mouse sitting in the park opposite the parish, in the gazebo we use to call Castle Grayskull. I went over to her. She faked a smile when I sat next to her. I could tell she just wanted to be alone. We didn't say anything at first. I wanted to give her a hug. 'I blew it back there, didn't I?' she said, just to break the silence.

'Can't be a proper rehearsal unless a fight break out,' I say.

'Yeah?' Mouse smiled, for real this time. 'Why do you say that?'

'Might as well fight now than fight in front the congregation.'

I expected her to laugh, but she purse her lips, furrowin her brow. I add, 'Rico have problems. We all learn never to listen to what he have to say.'

She folded her arms. 'Rico is certainly a boy I have to get accustomed to.'

'That's all right. We still getting accustom to him weself.'

She gaze over to the edge of the park, at the poui trees. 'Where I grew up, we had poui just like that. When I was little, I used to think that little rays of sunlight was trapped in the branches.'

'Where it is you grew up?'

'Back in Sun Canyon Road.'

Just then, Ti-Marie approach us. 'Sister Mother is lookin for you,' she tell Mouse. Then she look at me, 'And you! You have homework to do.'

Mouse nodded. As she was bout to get up, I had to stop myself from pullin her back down. I say, 'Ti-Marie, you ever study what Rico have to say?'

Mouse blushed. 'Jordon, I'm okay – '

'You feel I have time to listen to what that cuss-mouth have to say? My ears is not rubbish bins!' Ti-Marie then looked at Mouse. She pat her arm and say, 'Sister, Rico is a headache. Just relax and let it pass.'

★

That afternoon, I started *The Little Prince*. Read the whole damn thing before dinnertime. Take me just two hours. It's funny readin a book recommended by a person you admire. You feel like you start to know that person as you go along, wonderin which parts they marvel at, which parts make them sad. What became part of themselves. You get interested in fillin in the blanks. To really know somebody you need all the help you can get.

The first few chapters of *The Little Prince* was a mystery to me. The words was simple but the story was somethin else. I try my best at first to understand everything, but I couldn't deny that even by the end, I was still inside a maze. This is why I ain't like books much – books that people make up and nobody's round to provide a proper map. You feel like a dunce when you can't figure things out.

The book start off with a narrator, but you soon discover that the narrator don't take much part in the story. At the beginning, the narrator want to be an artist, but is told that he just not cut out for it. So he make his life as a pilot instead. As I say, narrator ain't much in the story – except in the beginning when he crash-land in the Sahara desert. He survives and lift his head up to see a little blonde boy, the Little Prince. The narrator describes the Little Prince as havin no hunger, no thirst, no fear. Was the Little Prince an alien? How could a normal child feel no fear in a situation like that?

Well, the Little Prince was fond of jumpin from planet to planet, meetin the people who live on them. These planets was real small. Most of them – only one person coulda live there. I imagine that some of them was no bigger than my bedroom in St. Asteria. Had this particular planet, said to be the smallest of all, that was home to a lamplighter. All he had was a street lamp. Nobody else live there, so there was no purpose to light the lamp. Yet the man used to light the lamp every evenin and put it out every mornin. And since the planet was so small, evenin and mornin was only seconds apart. Though he doesn't want to, he claim orders is orders, and he does his job.

Why not stop? What did he owe the street lamp that he feel he couldn't rest? Ain't have no choice but to go to Mouse with my queries. After dinner, as I help her clear the table, I ask her to explain the beginning to me. Her face turn bright pink. I think she had it in her mind that I woulda just forget the damn book and take a million years to admit it.

Well, the first thing she ask was what was my own thoughts on the lamplighter. Didn't help none because that was why I askin for an explanation. She wanted me to form my own interpretation of it first. She say when I give her that, she would give me hers. 'That is how we can learn from each other,' she say, poking my nose.

I know for sure that our little exchange make her day better. Life sometimes toss us what we need to get through the days. I like to think life toss me at Mouse. Make me think how a raindrop from the future could extinguish a fire from the past.

The next night, I dive right back into the book, from page one.

Had to read slow, so I couldn't finish it in one session, but I know that if I took it to school and use the lunch break I could finish it. It feel good to be doin somethin worthwhile, somethin that make the grownups proud. Never had much drive to do that before. I wasn't the type to stickfight with boys near the guard hut or gallop round playin scooch, dodgin cork balls left and right from boys too willing to make others cry. Not that I ain't like some of the outside children. Had nothin against most of them, but they was too loud for me. I could hardly keep up.

All of us at St. Asteria use to go to the same primary school, right in South, near San Fernando. That include Quenton and Rico, who was in their last year at the time, both slated to repeat exams come March. They fail the first time and so was banished to the limbo of *post-primary* – too dumb for secondary school, too old for primary school. When the news come in that they failed, Sister Mother put them on indefinite cleaning duty. Scraping muck and scrubbing grime, and scouring the oven with ammonia to dig out the scum.

Father Anton ain't never trust public transport, especially after seein how maxi-taxi conductors was makin it a hobby to hustle and harass schoolgirls. Well, so he say, but I know he just wanted to make sure everyone was accounted for after the final bell rang. He organize a van to get us to school and back home again – no unauthorized stops, no detours whatsoever. We wasn't allowed to go anywhere the van wouldn't go. On some days, he'd come too – take the head count himself.

That day, though, it was rainin real heavy. I was just there, sittin in the corner of the class, tryin to keep away from others, tryin to read and absorb the words. Miss Susan shut the blinds so none of the rain could blow in. Every time the lightnin come down and split the sky, the girls would scream out for their mothers while the boys banged the desks.

Through the storm, Miss Susan sat behind a stack of copybooks, diligently red-inking them with X's and ticks, mostly X's. But every once in a while, her eyes would glance up at me. She never pay me much attention before. Sometimes I think she forget I exist. That tend to happen. Teachers only remember the names of two types of students – the ones that coulda impress them, and the ones that coulda annoy them. Her eyes still on the books before her, she ask, 'You enjoying that?'

'I just tryin to understand it,' I tell her.

What she say after stick with me, 'Don't try too hard. Sometimes it's not bout the answers. Answers aren't important sometimes. Not as important as the questions.'

That burrow into my brain. But each question that come was like a scalpel, carving notes into my wooden brain. Couldn't make them connect up. The whole time, I feel like I was on the cusp of finding out something, but I couldn't get over the last ridge. It was like a sneeze that build itself up just to go back into hiding.

But the notion disappear that afternoon.

Was still rainin long after the last bell ring. The roads was flooded, and we was waitin for probably a half hour for the van to show up. Rico and Quenton had wander off somewhere. The rest of us was just sittin on the wooden steps of a classroom, huddling like we was posing for one of them old primitive cameras, daguerreotypes – waiting for our likeness to be sopped up on a metal plate. I wanted to finish the book, but everyone was talkin too much. Couldn't shut up bout end of term.

So, I sling my bag round my back, *The Little Prince* still in my hand, my thumb actin as a bookmark. I walk round to the back of the building, to the library and annex. Heard the rise and fall of heavy breathing. Curiosity get the best of me, so I went round to the back to see where the sound was comin from. There, Quenton was busy shovin his long, slimy tongue down some child's throat.

She wasn't fightin it. She was just strugglin to keep up with him. He had his hand up her skirt and although I couldn't see her face, I coulda see the peach panties too damn well.

Right before I turn to walk away – *whap!* I feel a hard slap on my shoulder. I spin round. Is Rico. Scowling like a dog. 'You like to peep, eh?' he say.

I try to get past him.

But he launch at me and grab my collar. He hiss, 'You lookin to try something like last time or what?' He make a fist and wave his knuckles in front my nose. He was expectin me to flinch but I didn't, and that just make it worse.

He snatch the book from me and start flippin through it. I

clench my teeth and the only word that coulda come outta my mouth was, 'Don't!'

Then I push him. Which was a mistake.

He hold the book up in the rain and start to rip out the pages. All I was seein was shadows now. Shadows in slow-motion, with the hiss of the rain spittin on my face and the wind blowin the pages across the schoolyard, into the puddles, into the runnels. I let out a howlin scream. Can't remember what I scream, or if it was just a roar. I just remember how I chase after them pages, them brightly coloured illustrations.

I seize the pages from the wind, stuffin them in my bag by the fistful. I remember catching a peep of everybody through the rain – and they was lookin back at me, probably wonderin if I finally lose it. Bats in the belfry again, boy. I stood in the middle of the yard, my eyes stingin, the rain leakin off my hair, runnin down my cheeks.

Ti-Marie dash through the pourin rain to retrieve me. She grab my shoulder and lumber back with me to the steps with the other children.

About two minutes later, the van was there, Father Anton in it. 'What on earth happened with you two?' he asked me and Ti-Marie when as he saw our wet uniforms. Ti-Marie just hang her head low, the rain still drippin from the ends of her hair. She glance at me, lookin to see if I'd say anythin. But I keep my mouth shut. And so did everybody else. I don't think Father Anton care much bout the wet uniforms, but the sudden tension amongst us raise a red flag.

'Somebody's going to have to speak up,' he said. But not even Ti-Marie would open her mouth for this one.

When nobody else say nothing, I swear Father was gon order the driver to pull to the shoulder so we could hold trial right there. He was good at noticing when something was wrong, but never good at finding out what. If you didn't want to tell him nothin, he'd respect your privacy. He understand that not all pain had to be public. He would just give you a look, nod and go back to business as usual. But you know it would torment him for the whole night through. And if you had half a conscience, it would damn well torment you too.

Rey finally speak up. 'The rain come down without warnin.'

Ti-Marie nodded. I didn't say nothin.

It rain that whole evenin. Up till dinner, I didn't say nothin. As usual, all of us sit round the big mahogany table and Sister Mother ask us bout the day. She always say that school was the fox's den. If we didn't learn anythin new that day, she would ask, 'Are you a goose? Am I sending geese to the fox's den?' She always went clockwise. She ask Rey, ask Nyla, ask Quenton, Elroy, Sookie, but she skip right past me and Rico, and go straight to Ti-Marie. When it was my turn, I couldn't reply. I could tell Rey was feelin it for me too. But no kinda sympathy coulda change what happen earlier that afternoon.

Before the evenin meal I try to piece together the pages I manage to save. But some was beyond all repair – text and illustration mushed together, the paper crumbling between my fingers, fragile like butterfly wings. Rey try to help out, but it was hopeless. After a half hour of gettin his hands sticky with glue and tape, Rey look at me and say, 'Jordon, boy, bite the bullet. The book gone-through.'

'We could fix it,' I say, still busying myself with the glue. 'You ain't gon help me?'

'I helpin you for the past half hour. It ain't make sense, boy.'

'Look, don't talk to me bout making sense. Just help me fix it.'

'Is just a stupid book.'

'But you know it ain't mine.'

'She'll buy another one. Is not your fault.'

During the meal, I squirm in my chair, fightin to give nothing away on my face as I ate my food, chewing the requisite seven times before each swallow. Kept my eye on my plate the whole time – couldn't bear to look Mouse in the eye. When dinner was over and Sister Kitty and Ti-Marie was clearin the table, Mouse pull me aside to ask me about the book. She knew, boy. She had to know. I couldn't hold it in no more. Everythin just stripped away. I prop my face against her small chest. And she wrap her arms round me. I close my eyes. I remember feelin her palm sweepin up and down my back.

Could hear her soft voice, could feel it washing against me. 'Tell me what upset you. Who upset you?' She wanted to repay me for the other day. Was then I realize we coulda be a team.

Between the sobs and hiccoughed words, I spill the whole thing – every damn detail. Told her bout what happen to *The Little Prince*. How I try to put it together again – like Humpty Dumpty. How I try, and fail. I blubber the whole way, keep sayin, 'I know I promise I wouldn't get no dog-ears on it.'

She didn't seem too sad bout it, but she was damn angry, I could tell. She tell me she was goin to talk to Sister Mother, and ten minutes later, Quenton and Rico was summon from their room. Sister Mother put them to sit on one side of the table. Me, Sister Mother, Bulldog and Mouse was on the other side. Was four against two.

Four grimaces versus two smiles.

Sister Mother oversee the whole thing, her eyes fixed on every nuance of my face until I was done laying my side out. Then her eyes shoot to Rico. She didn't even have to wait for him to confirm the story. The advantage of not bein a big talker is that when you do talk, people never assume you lie or exaggerate. 'Why would you do that, Jerrick?' she ask, her voice heavy with disappointment, 'Do you not realize the value of other people's property?'

Shruggin, he say, 'We was just havin fun.'

Bulldog shuffle in her chair, her world-renowned jowls dribbling outta her face. Although none of us coulda see it, we know she had the tambran whip hidden up her frock. Whenever a child had to *get it*, Sister Bernice 'Bulldog' Lafayette was the one to deliver. But this black knight of St. Asteria never swung unless Sister Mother give the nod. No matter if you was boy or girl, four or fourteen, innocent or guilty, if the call was put out for you to get it, you could bet your ass you was gon get it – signed, sealed and delivered. Nevermind your parents abandon you or gone forever – you do the crime, and it's tambran time.

No one ever know how she coulda hide that whip. She would pull that fucker out from *nowhere*. I ain't know whether she hid it up her habit or in the crevice of her cunny. I ain't know what compel Sister Mother to put this beast in charge of discipline. But, yes, anytime somebody was in trouble and Bulldog was there during the summons, shit was gon go down.

Quenton say, trembling, 'Rico didn't know it was Sister Maya's book.' I could hear his feet knocking against the legs of the table.

'It doesn't matter *who* the book belonged to,' Sister Mother shot back.

'Time runnin out,' Rico say.

'Pardon?' Mouse cut in, cocking her head..

Rico suck in some air.

The three sisters just look at him, silent.

'Time runnin out. So we just havin we fun.'

'You call what you did fun?' Mouse ain't try to hide her anger.

The wrinkles around Sister Mother's mouth deepened as she spoke, 'Fun is only fun when everybody involved is having it. Our lease on life is too short for you to be mucking about.'

Rico roll his eyes.

Sister Mother narrow her eyes at him. 'But what more can I expect out of a pig than a grunt? I get tired of speaking, and you just don't seem to hear. What is it the Trinis say? *Those who don't hear will feel?*'

Rico's face went pale that same time, figuring out fast the verdict and sentencing from this tribunal. He was now *eyeballin* me. Clenchin his fist as if to slam the table, but he bite his top lip and hold back at the last second.

Sister Mother asked Quenton, 'You didn't have any involvement in this tomfoolery, right?'

'No, Sister.' The boy was quick on the draw.

'Then you may go back to your room. You boys are lazy tailors tasked with long stitches.' She turn to Bulldog and give her the nod. 'Ten should suffice.' Bulldog return the nod, getting up from the table. It was only then I notice Sister Kitty peeking from the doorway.

'Wait!' Sister Kitty's voice rang out. She emerge from behind the wall. 'Isn't there a better way we could do this?'

Sister Mother narrow her eyes at her. 'Better way? Do you mean *your way*, Sister Katherine?'

Sister Kitty always picked up for Rico, with the claim that she coulda save him from himself. Every brutality has a history, every kick and every cuff had a deeper meanin. She liken him to a beaten pothound – beat the dog enough and it liable to turn on everybody. What he need is understanding, she say. Was love that would cure the boy. Was love that could kill the beast. But Sister

Mother wasn't one for that – the hug, the chin on the shoulder, the kiss on the forehead. Love, for her, was good old discipline, making sure you don't stumble on your way up that narrow staircase to Heaven.

Sister Mother say, 'There's a reason you weren't gathered here with us, Sister Katherine. I appreciate all of your good work, but being a disciplinarian isn't your forte. Sometimes I don't know what your method is aiming for – it feels like you wouldn't hit a crab in a barrel with it. There comes a time you have to admit a weakness to yourself, before others have to point it out to you.'

She turned to Mouse during those last words, as if it was a warning to her as well. Her eyes still fixed on Mouse, she ask, 'Perhaps Sister Maya can have her say, since it was her property that was vandalized.'

Mouse, sweating now, dropped her glance and nodded. 'The weed of crime bears bitter fruit,' she say, causing Sister Mother to raise her eyebrows. Mouse then put her chin up again and added, 'Let the boy have it.'

Sister Mother got up from her chair, saying to Mouse, 'Sister Katherine can learn a thing or two from you. If there comes a time some of these children would rather listen than feel, then I'm all for it. In the meantime,' glancing over to Bulldog, 'ten should suffice.'

Kitty's glare cut right through Mouse. The two prettiest nuns in Trinidad poised for a catfight – as I say, was this a prank or a miracle? Kitty didn't need to say nothin to show her fury. Them menacing, gimlet eyes was enough to get the message through.

'Come, runt,' Bulldog's mannish voice grumbled as she led Rico into her room.

He look at me, his eyes burning, and say, 'Take a good look.'

He hustled to unbuckle his pants, letting his trousers fall to his ankles, displaying his white drawers. He then pull his drawers down to his knees, his bare bottom and big balls hanging for everyone to see. He didn't have to do this – it was his way of saying *fuck you*. I remember the look of surprise on Mouse's face.

I, myself, never had to face that kinda wrath. As Mouse's eyes crept to me, a slight frown on her face, I could tell that it was in her mind to ask me if I ever did. I know it bother her. But I couldn't answer a question that wasn't asked. She close her eyes.

Then Bulldog shut the door.

★

The next mornin, we was all awakened by bangin and screamin.

'*I can't get out! I can't get out!*' It was comin from Mouse's room upstairs.

Everybody spring straight outta bed and gather at the stairs. We coulda see the room from where we was. Kitty was standing right before it. She reach her fingers towards the door and pluck out a couple of coins from the hinges.

All of us turn to Rico when we see the coins. This was Rico and Quenton's signature prank – a joke they use to play on the girls sometimes. They would tamp a stack of coins against the metal clasp of the door, stoppin it from pivoting and swinging open. Four bobs was all it take – they like to call it the *dollar door*. St. Asteria see its fair share of dollar doors.

Ti-Marie was givin Rico the death stare. Rey was smirking.

Rico put his palms up and say, 'Eh-eh, don't be lookin at me.'

Same time, the door swing open, revealing a puffy-faced, sweaty Mouse, her white nightwear in wrinkled disarray, hands still balled into fists, a few lank hairs hanging down in strings from her veil-matted hair. Kitty slip her into an embrace, pattin her back. Mouse's expression didn't change – eyes still bloodshot, lips quiverin.

Then Sister Mother come out from nowhere, adjusting her veil, eyes sharp on the scene. She shoot a stare at us and we knew to scatter. We bolt straight to the living room. I remained, in a daze, at the bottom of the stairs, my eyes fixed on Mouse, in all her vulnerability.

You know on them TV shows, the ones bout little boys growin up, there's always an episode or two where the boy locks eyes with a grown woman – not quite as old to be his mother, but still way outta his range. The woman walkin in slow motion, the sound-track swells, she turn to him, hair fallin over her eyes, and she give a smile, some sign of interest. Then it all flashes back to reality – everything crank back up to normal speed, the soundtrack back down to silence, her stern voice cuttin through the daydream: 'Are you there? Hello?'

I don't know if it happens with all boys, but I know it happen

39

with me. Mouse in slow motion. Mouse bathed in a lens flare. Mouse in time with the orchestra. Sounds strange to admit it, but I know how detached I was, even as a child. Seein other children hold their mothers' hands, bein propped up on the shoulders of their fathers made me realize a superfluity of nuns, no matter how dedicated or compassionate, just couldn't size up. I ain't never consider Mouse a real nun, though. Nuns never panic, not outward like that. They always had an unearthly resilience, like the world couldn't interfere with their head.

Rico get the blame, but I see who really do it, you know. I don't know why, but I ain't never tell a soul. Seen it while I was headin up the stairs to use the bathroom. Couldn't stand the one downstairs. Half them boys never bother to flick the light switch when they wake up to piss – they use to just waltz in and start streamin out pee, wiggling round until they hear it hit water. There was hardly a morning when the whole boys' wing didn't have to be moppin up the bathroom. Pee was pee, couldn't tell who was doin it, so it might as well been everybody was doin it. I know it wasn't me. As I say, I used the toilet upstairs, even though it was off limits.

That night, Sister Kitty come creepin outta her room same time as I hit the last step. I stop in my tracks, crouchin to observe her. She tiptoe cross the carpet and put the coins along Mouse's bedroom door. Swear I see it, this grown-ass woman, a lady of the cloth, pullin schoolboy pranks in the middle of the night.

It ain't surprise me. I know Kitty was capable of nastiness. She done a lot of good things in St. Asteria, but I could never trust her. I known Sister Kitty all my life – she was there when I first come. She was too nice sometimes, like that dishonest kinda nice. Like she had to have you look up to her for her to be nice to you.

I ain't sayin she was all fake. I think she genuinely meant it when she said she loved the children at St. Asteria. I think she woulda lay herself down on hot coals for some of us. Take a stroke or two from Bulldog, if she could. If I close my eyes, I can remember her pretty face perfectly. Every gentle groove, every deep crease. She would halfway make eye contact with me. Her lips would curve down slight. She'd go slack-jawed. Nostrils would flare. All of this would happen for just a second. A facial tic. But she couldn't hide it from me. Things wasn't right between us.

You see, few years back, I had dengue and Kitty was in charge to see over me. She interfere with me during that time. At the time, I ain't think much of it. Grownups could strap you to a chair and beat you when you're young and stupid, and you mightn't think much of that either. It's funny, the things you accept as good for you when you're little.

Didn't like to think much bout it, really. I was halfway outta it most of the time, anyway. Probably wasn't nothin. People had it worse. Sure if I tell somebody, they just gon tell me that, and that I need to get over it. Thinkin makes it worse, makes the past seem bigger than it is. It's best to think there's nothin to get too excited bout. But all of this is just to say I wasn't surprised about what I see Sister Kitty do.

The truth about the door was always on the tip of my tongue. One breath and one lap of the tongue away. But I couldn't do it. Didn't make sense. They done jail the wrong man for it, anyway. Kitty try to pin it on Quenton, but it was Rico alone who end up gettin the sentence. No way that trial was gon be challenged. Had no way nobody was gon admit they was wrong. Not now, and certainly not to Rico, who was on bathroom duty. The boy had to spend the weekend scrubbin the scum from the shower walls.

After, I wonder for a long time why I never say nothin. Funny thing was, when she went back to her room, it ain't even cross my mind to remove the coins. Maybe because I was half-asleep at the time, or maybe I wanted the prank to pull through, so I could see her get caught. Maybe I keep quiet just because I know there ain't a soul that'd take a child's word over a nun's.

3

'It's just going to add smoke to their minds.'

★

We used to have a Panasonic TV. A nice one, shaped like a box. We didn't get to watch it much except for Saturdays, though. Then one day, it blew. Just *zap!* Just like that. When Father Anton carried it to fix and got bombarded with all these terms – voltage spike, capacitor, diode – he just throw the blasted thing out. Sister Mother wasn't in no hurry to replace it. She believed the TV was replacing our conversations. To me, it was the opposite. It was good at bringin us together – though I don't think any of us prefer the sound of our conversations.

Two weeks later, one of the Sunday people donated a TV to us. But wasn't the same. This one was black-and-white, and it was small. And this was round the time when everything in the world still seem so big. I never woulda think they make TVs so small. *Xena* wasn't as heroic on it. *Fresh Prince* wasn't as funny on it. Shit, you couldn't even tell which *Mighty Morphin Power Ranger* was which! It had nothin to look forward to except eyestrain.

Few weeks after that, round Christmas vacation, Mouse get struck by an idea – a grand scheme. She saw an ad for an upcoming movie called *The Prince of Egypt*, an animated musical about Moses. We always wanted to go to the cinema, but Sister Mother and Bulldog was always against it. Bulldog flat-out used to call cinemas *sin houses*. Sister Mother never share *that* particular view, but nothin showin in any cinema never had any value – religious, cultural or intellectual. Her words, not mine.

So, in St. Asteria, we learn to hate movies. Hate them only because everybody else in school see them before any of we ever could. Worst thing in the world when people can't shut up bout something you could never experience. And by the time it come out on VHS, well, the rest of the world already move on. Movies was never as good as the other kids make them out to be, anyway.

Mouse gathered up the rest of the nuns before dinner to introduce the idea. I was on my way to the kitchen when I overheard the meeting. I stay round the corner to listen. The way how Mouse sounded, she wasn't goin to take no for an answer. When she went, she went prepared. She break it down: A major theatrical release based around one of the most famous Bible stories. A story about two princes of ancient Egypt. A movie, described and reviewed as a landmark of animation for its time, suitable for all ages. That was how she spoke. You woulda swear she was a writer pitchin the idea to a studio executive. You woulda swear she had money on the line.

As soon as she finish, Kitty jump in, 'Sounds fine. We'll rent it. They can watch it right here in the living room.'

'Watch it here? On *that* TV?' Mouse said. 'Think about the influence a Bible story on the big screen can have on them. Imagine how it will stay with them.'

'Does it remain true to the Bible's telling, though?' was Sister Mother's main concern. 'It *is* Hollywood, after all.' According to Sister Mother, Hollywood was design to poison and brainwash – you know how that kinda talk could go. To tell you the truth, listenin to children talk in school day-in and day-out coulda fuck up a mind much more than Hollywood ever could.

'It's just going to add smoke to their minds,' Kitty chime in.

'I'm certain there'll be some artistic license used, and there'll be a few inaccuracies,' Mouse reply, 'but that is why we're here, aren't we? This is part of our job, isn't it? To put everything into its proper place. To awaken the truth in them. So, if we plan to go, we'll accompany the children –'

'I want no part of it,' Sister Bulldog cut in.

Mouse said, 'That's okay. Not all of us have to go.'

'What do you think?' Sister Mother said. 'Think Sister Maya has something worth considering?' I couldn't believe Sister Mother was actually making an allowance for this. My heart was racing.

Kitty mumbled an okay.

'I'll consult Father Anton. If he sees no fault in it, then at dinner, we'll inform the children,' Sister Mother said.

And I'll tell you somethin, dinner never tasted so good in St. Asteria. Seasoned with good news, even Mac and Cheese coulda be banquet food. I couldn't even fathom watchin a movie on a screen twenty times bigger than me!

Me and Rey coulda barely sleep. We keep repeating the release date over as if it woulda make time go faster – December 18th. First show! December 18th. Surround sound! December 18th. Big screen! I probably had the date loopin in my head.

The buildup was half the fun. We had a calendar in the study and we cross off the days in red marker. During dinner, we was given reminders about Moses' life. Moses, son of Amram and Jochebed, brother of Aaron and Miriam, father of Gershom and Eliezer. Moses, they told us was known as Moshe, from the Hebrew word *masha*, which mean to draw out. Drawn outta the reeds from the Nile by the Pharaoh's daughter,

Raised as a prince. Fled as a criminal. Returned as a liberator.

We all took something from the story. *We* wanted to be taken in by the Pharoah, but we had to remember where we come from. We were loyal to our miserable pasts. They say you should rise up from the dust you was born in, but we could never really get it out from our clothes. In the oven used to mould mankind, we was born in the scraps of coal at the bottom, thinkin we owe somethin to the soot.

Suppose Moses felt like that once. Taken in by a King, the debt must have felt enormous. That's why God come down to speak to him. Tell him to work off what he owed. But even forty years of roamin the desert with a band of chatterin Israelites wasn't enough payment. Start where *we* are, life ain't somethin to live. It's somethin to pay back.

When December 18th finally come, we pack up in Father Anton's van and make our way to the noon showin. *The Prince of Egypt* was doubled with *Jack Frost*, but Jack Frost wasn't part of the deal, so the plan was to leave at the intermission.

Sister Kitty and Mouse agree to be our chaperones. Well, Mouse agree. Kitty get muscle into it. During the whole car ride, she ain't say a word. She remain huddled against the van door, peering out the window like a sulking child on a rainy day. Every once in a while, her gaze would drift over to Mouse, hunched up playfully next to Sookie and Ti-Marie. I knew, because my gaze was driftin over there too. It was jealousy. Bein loved makes you feel special – till you find out that person love everyone else just the same.

I suppose that's how Kitty feel when we show Mouse love. She probably thought our love was hers and hers alone.

Father Anton probably catch her mood from the rearview when he ask, 'Excited for the movie, Sister Katherine?'

'Been a while since I've been to the theatre,' she said, raising her chin at him.

Father Anton laughed. 'I'm sure it's still just a big screen and a projector.'

When we pull up to the front, we didn't expect to see so much people. They didn't even open the gates to the box office yet and the queue was runnin round the street corner. After we disembark, Mouse stick her head back in and ask Father Anton to join us. Wasn't so much an invitation, more a plea. She didn't want to be stuck with Kitty. But Father Anton just smile at her and say, 'Sister, would love to, but I have a lot of preparation for Sunday,' and take out his pocket Bible and start circling passages.

At the front of the building, at each side of the entrance, was the movie posters and their taglines. To the right, *Jack Frost*. To the left, *The Prince of Egypt*. To the side of the silhouette of Moses' face: *The Power is Real, The Story is Forever, The Time is Now*.

There was two boys, barely lookin eighteen, smoking in front of us. They make Sookie start coughin. Then a small group of middle-aged men cross the street wolf-whistled at Kitty and Mouse, but both of them remain quiet, pretendin to hear nothin. It was four men – look like they just stumble outta some bar.

Mouse kept us close together and shot a fiery look at them, but Kitty just spun in a half-circle and faced the wall, huggin herself, as if shielding herself from a blow. She looked very uncomfortable. I kept my eye on the men, wonderin how far gone you had to be to reach that point – to be suckin your rum-soaked lips at ladies of the cloth. A sudden stab of dread pulse way up in my throat. Quenton look like he was two seconds away from explodin.

But the men left without incident. Quenton lift the bill of his cap. His eyes didn't leave the men as they was walkin away. He wanted to fight. Don't know if it was to defend the sisters, or just because he wanted to slam some heads.

But when we finally make it into the cinema, we forget all bout that. Still, it wasn't how I expected it to be. The soles of my shoes threaten to pull off with each step on the sticky, grimy floor, and I swear I coulda see one of the maintenance men shooing a rat through the exit. Either a rat or a very big cockroach. The lights was still on, and the cinema screen was blaring a signcard tellin us to keep our surroundings clean – something the last set of patrons hadn't bother with. Had candy wrappers, popcorn packets and greasy napkins sprinkle all cross the floor.

We got tickets to the lower house section and end up wedged right under the ledge of the upper balcony. We was lucky to find a row for ourselves. I sat next to Sookie and Mouse. More and more people started filterin into the cinema and the chatter was non-stop. I catch it in small bursts. The mother behind me was tellin her child bout how his father is a damn liar. The girl in front of me kept remindin her boyfriend that she had to leave early. I coulda even hear the people two rows across, asking each other if they goin to parang later.

I felt nervous with all these people round me. Felt like I was in the wilderness. It was night and you could hear all the creatures round you. To calm myself, I looked up at the projector beam streaming faint over me. Through the beams was a curling twine of smoke, blowing over the balcony ledge and coilin right above us. Kitty took notice of it too. She turn to Mouse and whisper, 'Isn't it against the rules to smoke in the balcony?'

Mouse nodded. 'They're not supposed to be doing that. Should we tell somebody?'

'These people need to enforce the rules.' Kitty pursed her lips.

As soon as she said that, the lights began to dim. All our eyes immediately lock onto the screen, except Kitty's, who was still glaring at Mouse. A surge of shushes rise up from all sections of the cinema and the chatter slow down – it ain't stop, but it wind down to a low rumble.

Then the screen lit up and the title of the movie emerged from the dark before drowning in a mass of red fog. I wanted to burst out in applause at this alone. The first song ring in:

46

Deliver us, hear our call!
Slaves, whips cracking under the desert sun.
Deliver us, Lord of all!

Skin crinklin like paper, black towers of shaky scaffolds, large stone statues in the distance.

Remember us, here in the burning sand.

A scream, sharp like a banshee, fly cross the cinema. I didn't even know it was comin from right next to me. I jolt to my side.

Deliver us!

Sookie scream out again, her hand clamped over her eye. Everyone turn to watch her. Some suckin their teeth, some shushing her. One man bellow out, 'Cool yourself, small girl!'

There's a land you promised us.

Kitty lean over, stretchin across two seats before getting up. People gesture for her to sit down, groanin and cussin under their breath. She squeeze over to Sookie and lifted her hand from her eye.

Sookie was still cryin. 'It gone in my eye!'

Kitty look up at balcony, at the worm of smoke creepin up to the ceiling.

Deliver us to the promised land!

'It must be burning ash from a cigarette,' Kitty say, and she grab Mouse's shoulder and hiss, 'Knew this was a bad idea. We have to get her to a hospital.'

'What happened?' Mouse asked, frozen in disbelief.

'We have to leave! Now!'

Kitty start pullin every one of us outta our seats.

I ask, 'We can't stay and watch the movie?'

'How dare you ask that, Jordon?' Kitty say, yanking my arm.

Father Anton was waitin for us outside. We drove Sookie to the hospital, which wasn't far. None of us say anythin in the waiting room. Mouse went to the bathroom. When she come back out, I could tell she'd been crying.

The doctor say that Sookie suffer a very minor corneal abrasion from rubbing her eye. But what Kitty focus on was the little mark on Sookie's cheek. Sookie, fair of face, would be forever scarred. That was the big tragedy.

None of us coulda talk to the girl. At least not for a few days.

Wasn't her fault that the ash fall on her eye and cheek, but we couldn't stomach the fact that the day was ruined – especially when the mark disappear. The promised day.

We only feel bad for her when she feel like she had to apologize for the whole mess.

4

'Because I am a scorpion, you foolish frog.'

★

I ain't sure if the plan was to comfort us, or to comfort herself. On Christmas Day, Mouse give us a present we never coulda expect – a videogame console. A luxury. It was a second-hand Nintendo Entertainment System, come with *Super Mario Bros.* and *Duck Hunt* and two controllers. It shake the slump right outta us. As I say, funny how a raindrop from the future could snuff out a raging fire from the past.

When Kitty saw the gift, she just remind us that we had to get ready for Mass. Tell you that Mass was the longest in our whole lives. When it was over, we race cross the yard from the parish back to St. Asteria. Father Anton come along to see what all the fuss was bout. He even help set up the damn thing. When we turned it on, we just stare in awe as the 8-bit title screen come up. The only downside was that we had to play it on our small, black-and-white TV. But we didn't care. Rico and Quenton took the first turn. Might as well – the rest of us was too nervous to go first. Bold hands was required to christen the controllers.

While they was playin, Father Anton turn to Mouse and ask, 'You bought this?'

Mouse looked happy. Struck with relief, as if a cancer diagnosis come in negative. 'Wasn't much. It's an old system.'

Father Anton laughed. 'Well, this is totally new to them.'

We didn't budge from the TV for the entire day. Later that afternoon, Rey and I was taking turns at *Duck Hunt.* The game was simple. To play, you had to point this plastic gun at the TV screen and shoot the ducks before they fly away. Somehow, the TV coulda register the position you was shootin at. I could hear Kitty marchin back and forth behind us. 'It's training them to be violent,' she was saying to Father Anton. 'I read about these things. They desensitize children to violence.'

'Sister,' he reply. 'They're shooting ducks.'

'Please understand –'

He laughed. 'They're shooting digital ducks with a plastic gun.' And that was the end of that conversation. But it stay with me.

The bitch really start punishing Mouse for gainin our respect. Whenever it was Mouse's time to cook, Kitty refused to eat. Suddenly, the food had too much salt. The chicken didn't have no chadon beni. The rice too soggy. You woulda swear we was accustomed to eating eleven secret herbs and spices every meal. Not only that, she used to grab Mouse and smooth out any crinkles in her habit. It was just an excuse to manhandle her. Her favourite line was, 'You think that's worthy of the veil?'

Fights started happenin because of the games. That's what happens when you have eight children and two controllers. Naturally, it was Rico who was the first to fuck up the scene. He would get Game Over after Game Over, and insist that the game was cheatin him. He'd drop into pits, fall into lava, run into enemies, and then cuss for the whole house to hear. Sister Mother threaten to take it away if this disorder continued. But in the end, Mouse just convince her to ban Rico from playing it.

The next morning, when we woke up, the Nintendo wouldn't work. Everyone blame Rico, but I know who really do it. Before we even discover what was wrong, Kitty come up and say, 'A rat must've chewed it.' We didn't even know the power wires was damage then. She just assume we already discover that. But wasn't no rat chew that wire. The cut was too clean – knife-clean. Naturally, all blame went to Rico. And just like with the dollar door incident, Kitty let Rico take the fall.

The bitch was evil. She coulda be a fuckin La Diablesse for all I know.

This was why we couldn't have nice things. Mouse didn't talk much after that. And when she did, she spoke with a slow drawl, pushin the words out one by one, as if they was great weights, as if she was just bidin her time. I went up to her room one day. I know I was forbidden, but I couldn't lay it to rest. I had to say somethin. She didn't seem to care bout any regulations, though. When I knock on the door, she let me in.

In a minced mumble, I say, 'Sorry bout what happen.'

She shudder a bit as if the memory jolted her. 'I tried,' she say.

'Is just Rico's nature to be wicked,' I tell her.

She click her tongue and sat on the bed. 'People aren't meant to be wicked. People aren't scorpions.'

'What that mean?'

She was shaking her head. 'Sorry – it's just a story.'

'Tell me bout it.'

She say, her words dripping slow, 'I don't know if it's appropriate, Jordon.'

'I wanna hear.'

With several clearings of her throat, she start off. 'So, a scorpion comes across a river and cannot swim but needs to get to the other side. He comes across a frog and asks for his help. *Lemme ride on your back*, the scorpion says. *The swim is not far. You'll be doing me a great favour.*'

'The scorpion wouldn't sting the frog?'

'Right. Exactly what the frog was thinking. So, naturally, the frog is doubtful, but then he thinks about it and realizes that he's safe. Because if the scorpion stings then the scorpion will die as well. So the frog agrees to take the scorpion across the river. The scorpion hops on and the frog begins to swim across. Halfway there, the frog feels a piercing stab in his back.

'*Now we will both die!* the frog says in utter disbelief, *Why would you do this, Mr. Scorpion?* To which all the scorpion could say was, *Because I am a scorpion, you foolish frog.*'

'So both of them die?'

'It was the scorpion's nature to kill. But people aren't scorpions.'

I say, 'Is the scorpion who was the fool.'

'How so?'

'He shoulda wait. You know, till he cross the river.'

'Sting the frog after he got to the other side?' For a moment, she was silent in thought. 'I suppose we can look at it from a different angle and say that the frog killed the scorpion. Maybe the frog knew the scorpion would sting him. The frog sacrificed itself to ensure that there was one less scorpion in the world.'

'I ain't know bout that,' I say. 'But the scorpion didn't have no sense of timing.'

'I've never thought of it that way.' She paused, and then she hug me. I live in that moment for years, boy. I take it and put it in my pocket. Then she said, 'You should go. You're not supposed to be up here.'

The next day, she was gone.

Sister Mother inform us that Sister Maya Madeleine Romany exited the front doors of St. Asteria in the predawn hours of the saddest day of our childhood.

St. Asteria stifled Mouse. I could imagine it was like breathing through a moist dishrag, day in and day out. Coulda see it in her face. The fierce lustre in her eyes going dim. What had happen in the cinema that day, as disappointed as we was, nobody take it harder than Mouse. She shuffle her feet round St. Asteria like some shellshock war patient. She was pale. Anaemia kind of pale.

Remember the dollar door incident? See, wasn't the actual door that cause Mouse to lose control like she did. I realize this later. It was the door to her life being jammed shut. That shit was what sprung the bedlam that mornin. Being trapped with children with junkie mothers and deadbeat fathers and haunted by phantoms. Didn't have no saints hiding beneath the rubble.

I couldn't get her outta my thoughts, outta my dreams. I couldn't say or do nothin bout it. I knew I'd get teased for it. Small man Jordon have the hots for a nun? Boy, I woulda never hear the end of it. Whatever I had for her, I had it bad. She used to sing in the shower and I woulda hang round the stairs just to hear it. Singin them old songs, but there was one I coulda tell she like the most. A peppy song that I never known the name of, starts off, 'If I had a hammer, I'd-a hammer in the mornin, I'd-a hammer in the evenin...'

I hummed it all the time, hoping she woulda notice. She did, once, and she did nothin but smile. She was good at dividing up her time with everybody. She did it so that nobody would feel special. She did it, I realise, so that she could distance herself.

The upstairs room was lock once again – it went back to being the Sealed Cave. I ask Quenton to help me break into her room. When he finally pry the door open, I ain't never felt so dismal. The walls look like some kinda skin disease – half of the paint did already flake off. The cobwebs and dust was back already. My mind cut back to the hours we spent breakin our backs scrubbin and moppin that floor.

Like nobody had live in that room at all. I hobbled round it, my eyes dashin round the whole room, fallin on every empty shelf and drawer. I search desperately for some kind of pattern. Like there was some riddle to be solve, and if I coulda solve it, she woulda come back. I was hoping she woulda leave at least one of the seashells behind – whether it was by mistake or intention – like treasure for me to discover. Not one stray hair. Nothin. Quenton hiss at me, 'What you doin, boss? Hurry up or we ass is grass!' I left the room and Quenton closed the door.

I ask Sister Mother if I coulda call Mouse on the phone, but she just gave me a glum look and say, 'I am here for you if you want to talk.' The fuck? – I didn't want to talk to Sister Mother, or nobody else.

I felt like somebody had died and I didn't get enough time with them. There was so many things I still had to talk bout.

-5-
'Why?'

★

Few months later, sometime round Easter, we went on a field trip to the Pitch Lake in La Brea – first time I been there. Ti-Marie sat next to me on the bus. Every once in a while, her arm would touch mine and she'd trace her fingertips along the warm nook of my elbow. As we drove along the last potholed road, the Pitch Lake finally come into view.

I remember just standin on the edge of it in awe as the guide recite its history. Kept stressing that Sir Walter Raleigh ain't discover shit – that the Pitch Lake was here for a long time before his British ass stumble upon it. Then he went all the way back to how the pitch was just decayed animals and plants and soils from millions of years ago. And that was all it was, the result of time and pressure. When we walked on the pitch, we was walkin on birds and mora trees and manicous, snakes and howler monkeys.

And people.

I remember how grey the sky was that day. Not like it was settin up to rain, but like the sun wouldn't bother much with this day. The guide look as old and black as the pitch itself, as malnourished and desperate as the scrubby land around it. Ready to join all the other things that would fall victim to time and pressure.

During the ride back, Ti-Marie sat next to me. 'We should talk more,' she say.

'Why? I ain't got nothin to offer.'

'Offer?' She raise her eyebrows at me. 'Well, if that is how you thinkin, I ain't have nothin either. You ain't understand that's not how friends work?'

'No, I mean it in a different way.'

She shake her head. 'Lemme tell you somethin bout the way of the world.'

I snort. 'The way of the world, girl? Who you hear this ole talk from?'

'Shut up!' She laugh. 'I hear it from somebody, okay? But that don't mean I can't talk bout it. Look, if you ain't have nothin, and I ain't have nothin, then we have got nothin to give each other but weselves.'

'So you gon give yourself to me, eh?'

'Aye, that's somethin people hardly get in this world.'

'I guess.'

'Better appreciate it.'

I remember that this was round the time Rey take a special liking to Jeannine. A crowbar couldn't pry his eyes off that girl. He tell me how she end up here. Jeannine's father smashed his head against the dashboard. Everyone involved in the crash survive except him. The mother crawl outta the burnin wreck and right into bed with another man who end up choppin her hand off with a cutlass. She end up bleeding to death. The man end up in Golden Grove Prison and Jeannine end up in St. Asteria.

Justice served.

But wasn't Jeannine told him this. It was Rico. When I hear that, I ain't say nothin, but I was ashamed of Rey.

Me and Rey was gettin our first chest hairs at that time. But Rey's hormones raged harder than mine. He'd be touchin himself through his pants when he thought nobody was watchin. Not masturbating. Just touchin. He use to sleep with his pants off, and hold the pillow against his crotch at night, and he had a pair of granny panties and a bra. He say he get them from Rico. I ain't even say nothin bout that – I just look at him like, what the fuck? And he use to lay them out on the bunk, panties below and bra above, as if an invisible woman was sleepin in the bed, and just gawk at them with this drugged, distant look in his eyes.

I ain't gon lie and say that shit ain't disturb me.

Since Mouse was gone, I never see Kitty so happy. She probably get on her knees and thank God for it every night. This time round, it seem she was puttin in work to win back our respect.

Near the church steps, she and Father Anton clear out a space and roll out some chairs in a circle with a bundle of sticks and ash at the centre. She call this the *Feu de Joie*, which we just get to callin the Joyfire. This was round the August vacation. On the weekends, during dinner, with our plates on our laps, comfortably barefoot, we'd go down by the Joyfire and she'd toss a match in it – ain't know if she ever needed a permit to do that, but there it was, bright and burnin. We'd sit round it, shovellin coconut bake and fry-dry into our mouths. Kitty would strum the guitar and sing songs while we ate. Sometimes we even get to choose the tunes. If they was appropriate.

No matter what she do, though, she could never get my respect. I hated her more and more as the months went by. Thing is, I didn't want to hate nobody. I ain't never really hate nobody before this. Once I started feelin it, though, it took over.

And Kitty wasn't stupid – she knew. I was the one who wouldn't look her in the eye. I was the one who wouldn't forgive. She call out to me one night at the Joyfire, 'Pick a song, Jordon.' I didn't want to pick no blasted song.

But she was persistent. 'Jordon? Any requests?'

Everyone was lookin at me. She start again, 'Jordon –'

'If I Had a Hammer,' I end up spittin out. That was a mistake.

'Very good, I actually know that one.' She start with the first few chords and then pick up the pace. When the lyrics start to pour out, I clench my teeth. Kitty had done gone and pour too much sugar to the blend and turn it into a sing-along. She was pluckin and twanging away on that guitar, urging every man jack to clap along with it. Singin it like this had to be a sin.

Dinner, music and firelight – you'd think that woulda be enough, right? Well, after the songs, we had to tell stories. Any kinda story, but it was usually scary stories, just boogieman-kinda-scary, not real-life-shit-kinda-scary. We was told that we was safe in the Joyfire. Nothin coulda get to us there.

Quenton would kick off with a story bout some shit he see on *X-Files*, like tentacles bustin out of a man's chest, or dead children rising up from the grave. Jeannine would just re-enact stuff from books she was reading at the time – mostly Enid Blyton. Rey would take stories from the Bible and set them in modern time – if the water turned to blood, if the first-borns suddenly start dyin, if the rains one day never cease.

Was Ti-Marie's turn that night. She draw her stories from dreams – two of them. Although I was actually listenin, I can't remember some of the details, but I can recall what they was about, or at least how I had picture them in my own mind.

The first dream was in a desert. I didn't imagine the desert during the day, though. It was a dark blue kind of cold. In the middle of this desert was a big castle, like a sand fortress with big red pennants on each corner tower. The desert stretch on for miles with nothin else in sight. Not a cactus, vulture or bone to be seen. There was a piano in the fortress. A man was playin it with not a care in the world. He was playin beautiful music, she say. As she approach him, he vanish – *poof!* – as did the fortress and the music. That was the first dream.

The second dream was bout a girl who roam the desert. Not sure if it was the same desert, but I was imaginin it was. This time, it was day, bout noon or so. Scorchin hot sun. She was weeping. The girl's throat was so parched that she couldn't even crack a sound while she wept. Each tear that fall to the sand sprout a flower. Ti-Marie say that they was white flowers, but I like to imagine that they was red roses. A young, black girl walkin along the dunes with a trail of small red roses behind her. It just seem more fittin that way.

When she was done, she was quiet for a moment. The fire reflected off her dark skin – forming a fine sheen like on lacquered wood. Everybody was silent as the fire crackled, sparks flickerin round her like candleflies. There shoulda been somethin, some response to what she dream. But the words wouldn't come. We just sat in our places, nodding, sayin nothin. Perhaps the fact that nobody dare to crack a joke was flatterin enough. But I felt bad bout the silence. Felt bad bout mostly everything them days.

I'd wake up at random moments in the night and head outside. I'd scale the parish fence and sit near the blackened wood-scraps of the Joyfire. It was usually cool and quiet, just the crickets for company. I'd lie flat on the grass, starin up at the church spire, at the clouds looming behind it. I imagined the Little Prince hopping from star to star, grippin tight onto a rope that branched off into twenty different directions – a bird at the end of each offshoot, flappin and hoisting him through space.

One night, I notice a cat sprawled off by the fence. It was dead. Its neck was broken. Another one come up to me – a black and white stray cat – purring and rubbin itself up against my side, circling me and whiskin its tail in short, sudden curls. Then it stop right by me, purrin again. As I went to pat its back, its body suddenly went stiff and it hiss at me, flashin its teeth. Shiny fangs in the dark.

I bat it away and it scamper off.

I picked up the dead cat and hid it near the steps of the church. I just wanted a reaction. I wanted the Sunday people to see it. I wanted them to cry jumbie! Wanted them to cry lagahoo! Cry all manner of duppy that coulda haunt this place. But when we was ready for Mass, the cat was gone, and nobody ever say shit bout it. I don't like to think that someone move it. I like to think it's still out there – resurrected like Jesus. But whatever happen, it was clear: dead cats with broken necks wasn't part of the sacraments.

★

Few days later, Sister Kitty bought us some new sketch pads and colour pencils. Draw something that's on your mind, she tell us. I refused to draw Mouse, even though she was the only thing I coulda think bout. I was afraid to see how she woulda turn out just from my mind's eye. Distorted lines and mismatched facial features. She didn't deserve it. I coulda never capture her on paper – not even now.

So I drew Ti-Marie's dream instead, back at the Joyfire – the second one. The girl with the tear-sprouted roses in the desert. Ti-Marie's face look like it was gon burst when she see the picture, boy. She love it – couldn't stop talkin bout it. So, I give it to her. Later that day, Sister Kitty come up to me as I was sweepin up the front of the church.

She say, 'You did a great thing this morning.'

Anything for forgiveness. Anything to be in my good graces.

She had a little tub in her hand. In the other, she had a cord of wire fashioned into a loop at the end. She blew into it and a stream of bubbles flutter out the other side. Some of them look like they had tiny rainbows in them. She dip the loop into the bottle again and blew into it again. This time there was more bubbles.

'Was just a drawin,' I tell her.

'A startling number of people go their whole lives without having someone make something for them,' she say, her smile fading a little. She ruffle my hair and handed me the bottle and the loop. 'Try it,' she say.

'I don't want to.'

'Come on, Jordon.'

I dip the loop in the bottle and blew gently, but just one bubble come creepin out. A premature baby. A scrawny thing, strugglin to make its way into the world. It crawl through the air, as if it was a soul searchin for bone and flesh. It dwindle and dwindle and dwindle, until, *pop*, it was gone.

'Happy?' I said, and went back to sweepin.

I see Elroy sneak outta his room one night. I ain't never before talk to Elroy much. Nobody never really bother with him, and he never really bother with nobody. Most of the time, you forget the boy even exist. I used to wonder if he prefer it like that. Once again, it hit me how weird it was to be livin with people for my entire childhood and ain't really knowin some of them at all. I follow him and see his bulky shadow leanin forward against the fence, arms extended with the palms grippin tight to the wire, kinda like a reverse crucifix.

'Elroy, boy,' I say as I approach him, so he wouldn't be startled by my shadow.

He turn round. 'Mmm…'

'What you doin out here?' I ask.

'What you say me and you bust outta here?' he say. I know he didn't mean scalin no fence, because Elroy was too damn fat for that. Sister Mother say that he had a bad metabolism. Bad genes, inherited from parents who dump his ass off in a hospital car park when he wasn't even a year old. He was the only one who coulda take Rico one-on-one and really give him a good lickin. But, as I say, nobody never bother Elroy and Elroy never bother nobody.

Usually the boy's lips would be pushin out in a constant pout, but this time they was ajar the whole time.

'Bust outta here?' I say, laughing.

'Take some of the money they hidin in their bedroom, bust open the lock and never look back,' he say.

'Never look back, eh?'

'Yeah. Never look back.' The boy was serious.

'And then how we gon get to school?'

'School?' He turn to me, lookin at me like I was stupid. 'Fool, that is like breakin outta the pound to go back to the kennel.'

'So… where exactly we goin?'

'I ain't think *you* goin nowhere. You stayin right here. You ain't ready yet.'

'Elroy, what the hell you talkin bout?'

'Fool, what you think goin to happen to all of we? You think we gon remain in St. Asteria forever?' My stomach hurt when he say that. 'You think them always gon want to be there for we once we get old like dog? Nah. We gon find weselves alone. With nothin. And I ain't want to be here when that happen.'

'Why you sayin that? They won't do that.'

'Have nothin here, boy. Have to take care of weself.'

'Elroy, what the hell you think it have out there?'

'World movin forward. We can't stick!'

'That don't make any sense.'

'Suit yourself.'

I just walk away and went back to bed. I couldn't sleep at all that night. What he say was true. One day, it was all goin to come crashin down. Truth was, all of we here was keepin reality one step behind and it was goin to backstab us at some point. St. Asteria was a dream, and the hour would come when we all woulda have to wake up. Maybe I was already waking up. Mouse was already just another phantom. The Sisters was goin to have to let us go one day and a batch of new puppies would come in and replace us. And we'd be alone. In the dark. With nothin.

Nothin but plenty of time. And pressure.

★

In the parish, there was a small room used for Sunday school. We name it the Bubblegum Room, because it was painted a soft pink. You coulda see it from the chancel. If we wanted to talk to Father Anton or one of the nuns, they would just take us to the nave. If it was a very private matter, they would take us to the Bubblegum Room. I suppose it was a fittin name – cause from what I hear, talkin bout problems like chewin bubblegum. It ain't make nothin easier to digest.

You was always encourage to find your identity. Not borrow one from the outside, but release the one caged up inside you. But talkin to anyone from the church, you realize it ain't so much bout personal truth as it is bout livin the way *they* want you to live. Or thinkin the way *they* want you to think. You didn't have to be smart to realize this. When your problems could be dumbed down to verses and hymns, you grasp how useless talkin really is. Like chewin bubblegum.

I show up early for choir rehearsal one day. I wanted to be away from everyone for a while. The Bubblegum Room's door was slightly ajar. I peek in and I see two figures.

Rico and Sister Kitty.

And they wasn't talkin. He was on a chair and she was sitting opposite to him. His pants was dangling from his ankle, like a slave's foot shackle. She was jerking him off. Hard. I thought I was dreamin. A sight that nobody else would believe. It coulda be possession… voodoo… obeah, but Jesus Christ, even I thought my eyes was lyin at first. I ain't even know how it coulda get to that stage. Who tackle who, for how long, and how many times – it ain't matter. Once was enough to seal the deal.

But the question remain – *why* was she doin this? I thought bout it real hard. I couldn't even sing for the choir rehearsal.

God gave me the opportunity and I took it. I went to Father Anton the next day. I met him at the church nave and we sat in the front pew. I thought hard bout what I was gon say. If I just describe what I see, Kitty coulda turn the tables and claim that Rico force her. This was an actual possibility. I couldn't risk it. No, to bring the dragon down, I had to martyr myself.

'Sister Katherine came up to me last night,' I told Father Anton, cautious standard English coming out. 'She brought me to that room,' and I pointed to the Bubblegum Room, 'and she told me to close my eyes. Next thing I felt was my pants sliding down. Then she put… my penis… in her mouth.' The whole time I kept wonderin which passages would be the best reply to this story, which collection of verses would be most relatable.

Father Anton's mouth slowly drift open. I continued, 'She brought Rico too – '

'Wait, wait. You *and* Jerrick?'

I give him a nod. 'Both of us, yeah. I pulled away from her and told her that I didn't want to do that. So she turned to Rico instead and she was doing the same thing to him. She told him to be quiet and just enjoy it.'

He didn't say anything. He just put his palm on his forehead and exhaled sharp. 'Was this the first time?'

'No. I wasn't goin to tell anybody but – '

'No. No, Jordon. It's good you came to me.' Father Anton was noddin with each word.

'I don't want her to get in trouble – '

He spat out, 'This is *inexcusable* – '

'I hope I didn't – '

'Stay here.'

At a feverish pace, Father Anton went to fetch Kitty. He was fuming – and he didn't bother to hide it. It was scary, seein the old man like that. My heart was beatin fast. I gazed up at the crucifix. They tell me to always do the right thing. This was it.

Father Anton soon come back with Kitty and Rico. I remember them standing at the door, unable to push themselves to reach the pews. They was two blurred pillars, stiff against the sunlight. The house of the Lord wasn't havin them. Kitty finally made the first step forward. She look like she was minutes away from gettin slam with a death sentence. I remember Rico's look of utter confusion as his eyes turn to me. Still, I think he knew what was gon go down.

Father Anton ain't waste time. He ask Rico straight away bout his relations with Sister Kitty. We was in our own lil Joyfire here. He say that all he had to do was answer the question, tell the truth. And he did tell the truth. At the end, he let out two furious words: 'So what!'

Father Anton look like his head woulda explode. Kitty covered her face. Rico then throw in, 'Wasn't a frequent thing.'

Rico slump over, with his head hanging down, his fingers interlocked at the nape of his neck. Kitty's eyebrows quiver, her lips tremblin. I never before notice the colour of Kitty's eyes – a dark golden sheen, deep-set against the pallor of her cheeks. She was a terrified animal. All she coulda say, in a raspy breath, was, 'Lord, forgive me.'

'So the accusations have validity,' Father Anton say.

'Yes.' Kitty shake her head. 'Father, it wasn't out of malice. It was our way to connect. It helped him.'

Father Anton look like he wanted to cuss. 'Fondling thirteen year old boys was your way to connect, Sister? Are you hearing yourself?'

'Thirteen? Father, I'm fifteen,' Rico say, his voice fading at the end, suddenly realizing the ruse. As did Kitty. Both their eyes fell upon me. I sat up straight, chin up, grabbing my knees.

'I never touched Jordon, Father,' she said. 'I'd never do that.'

Rico cut in, 'Yeah. That part is a fuckin lie!'

'So you admit that everything else is true?' Father Anton say.

Kitty nodded, too weak, too ashamed to say yes. 'Father, if you can understand the situation with me and Jerrick in context, you would see what little sense Jordon's allegation makes. Jordon,' she mutter, 'Jordon, you need to tell the truth. Please, you know better.'

'Sister, listen to yourself –' Father Anton lifted his hand.

But Kitty cut him off. 'Jordon, let him know I didn't lay a finger on you.'

I say, 'I'm sorry. I didn't mean to tell.'

'Jordon… Why? Why are you doing this?'

Why, she ask? Why, she want to know?

There is only one answer.

Because I am a scorpion, you foolish frog.

6

'People only remember you at your worst.'

★

That evenin, Father Anton leave Sister Mother to sort out the business with Kitty. He pack me and Rico in his van and drive off.

'Where we goin?' Rico keep askin. I suppose he had it in mind we was bein ship off to some home for molested children, if there was such a thing. Shit, I was thinkin the same. I wonder if I'd made a big mistake.

But Father Anton didn't say nothin. Some old kaiso was playin on the radio. After bout ten minutes of driving, he say, 'You want me to change the station? You like this kinda music?'

I didn't say nothin. Rico neither. Father Anton say, 'If you want to listen to that dancehall and reggaeton garbage, just tell me.'

But we still didn't say nothin. He just keep on drivin. After another long silence, he say, 'You know *Jack and the Beanstalk*, right?'

'Yeah,' I say.

'Jack spent all his money on the magic beans and his mother threw them out and then they sprouted a beanstalk, right?'

Rico and I look at each other.

'And then he climbs up the beanstalk and he goes into the giant's house. *Fee-fi-fo-fum* – all of that. And he gets the golden goose that lays golden eggs. Kind of a weird story, eh? Usually these children's stories have some kinda moral. But instead we get some mumbo-jumbo bout magic beans.'

His eyes lock on us in the rearview. 'When do these magic beans actually work? I thought bout it one night. Sometimes I feel like it's my job to make sense of things. See, we try to plant magic beans in your backyards everyday, hoping one will sprout into a beanstalk. But the sad truth is that most of them are duds. You go out with your watering cans and water them seeds and you take your fertilizer and apply it day after day and nothing comes out. Because it's a dead seed. A dud.' He was quiet for a while.

'Sister Katherine gon get in trouble?' I ask, just to break the silence.

Father Anton fix his eyes on me again in the rearview. 'We probably won't be seeing her again.'

'Leave her alone, 'Rico say. 'She ain't do nothin wrong.'

'She ain't do nothin wrong?' Father Anton repeated, mock-ingly. 'Sexual Offences Act. Where a female adult has sexual intercourse with a male person who is not her husband and who is under the age of sixteen years. How old are you, Jerrick?'

He twist his mouth. 'Fifteen.'

Father Anton continued, '*Under the age of sixteen years*, she is guilty of an offence, whether or not the male person consents to the intercourse.' He then look in the rearview, directly at us. 'And is liable on conviction to imprisonment for five years.'

I ask, 'The police comin for her then?'

Father Anton remain quiet until we hit another traffic light. 'I was reading the papers today. Headline was about a man, shot his girlfriend, set her on fire. All in the name of love. Skim four pages down, there's a story bout a man saving a woman from a house fire. Why's that? Why's that man not the main headline?'

'Doesn't sell papers,' Rico say.

'*Correctamundo*,' Father Anton say. 'Road fatalities, corrupt politicians, campus rapist, the works. All headline material. But this is nothing new.'

'We have to highlight the bad so we don't repeat history,' I say, Sister Mother's exact words spillin outta my mouth.

But he just shake his head, 'History? People only remember you at your worst.'

We cross into a small town. I look at the people outside the window. People shufflin about, sidesteppin fruit vendors' feet on the pavement. A police officer blowin her whistle, directing traffic at a junction. The evening sun washing over the buildings. Father Anton was still goin on, 'You know what they say bout natural disasters? Earthquakes, hurricanes, tsunamis, volcano eruptions? They call them acts of God.'

He pause to turn at a junction, and then continue, 'They say these things happen because God's trying to maintain the status quo. Population control. When someone dies, they leave behind an entire future of resources. Food. Water. Employment. Animals kill each other and we just call it the food chain. The balanced ecosystem. So… what are we doing? What are we doing, fellas? What are *we* doing? *We* are the imbalance here.'

'What you talkin bout? Humans just can't go and kill each other,' Rico spit out.

'Why? Aside from the Commandments, why? If we look at the big picture, world hunger is more suffering than a quick murder.'

'Because then we gon just be animals!'

'Animals know how to take care of themselves. *Other* animals. *We* don't. What is the difference between humans and other animals, Jerrick? Tell me.'

'We more intelligent,' I answer for him.

'How so? Animals don't waste their resources. We do. We destroy our own ecosystem. Animals don't. No, no, no, son. The difference between animals and humans is that humans desire. Humans desire things that they don't need. What happens when a human's wants and needs are two different things?' He turn a corner. 'We get headlines in big bold red about a man killing his girlfriend in the name of love. God help us all. God help me if the people have to read about yet another servant of God molesting children. It's not going to happen, so help me, Lord. It is *not* going to happen.'

Rico's eyes was moist with tears. Saw it for just a split second before he pretended to be shading his eyes from the sun. We was drivin for about an hour and a half before the coconut trees started to appear, their long shadows blown across the narrow road. They stood parallel to each other, some bowing to us as we rode past, like giant earthworms burstin out of the ground.

Me and Rico had our eyes on the sea. I don't know if he ever saw it. But I never did. Jesus, it was like a dream. There it was – that band of muddy brown, baby-blue and mucky white, lookin like old washing machine water stretchin towards the horizon. Drove past a series of brokedown brick houses – salty remains of ancient beach-temple ruins.

We keep drivin. We take backroads until the beach was gone,

until all that was left was bush and a single dirt track that wasn't meant to be driven on. But we was drivin along it, anyway. We stop smack in the middle of it. Father Anton lit up a cigarette and blew a wisp of smoke out the window. I caught his eyes watchin me through the rearview again. He shut off the ignition. He say with a chuckle, the cigarette wagging from the corner of his lips, 'You know where we are?'

'Where?' Rico ask, his voice heavy with unease.

'You might think we're lost. But I know where we are. Once in a while you'll come to a place…' Father Anton blow out a puff of smoke. 'Everybody stumbles across this place. And it doesn't sit still. It doesn't have a home. It's like an animal that goes to sleep and wakes up and walks around before going back to sleep again. But no matter which direction we go from here, it would be the right way, fellas.'

'What the hell you talkin bout?' Rico ask. He look like he wanted to kick the driver's seat.

Father Anton turn round. 'You're going to come across this place and you're going to think you're lost. Ain't no road here. And you might want to backtrack and see if you find old things you once knew. Little landmarks. A big dinner table. A double decker bed. A primary school. That would be the only wrong way to go. Nobody lives backwards.' He took another drag.

He was facing front again, his eyes on the rearview. 'Life is only lived in forward motion. Have no other way to live but forward. The rest is a waste of damn time.' He turned the ignition and we drove on, even past where the dirt road stop, and we eventually end up back on the road, facing the beach once again.

He pulled up next to the remains of a brick house. Wet, jagged granite, rusty nails and coarse sand grains was scatter across the floor. Roof completely gone, stairs leadin up to nowhere.

Father Anton got out the car, flick his cigarette on the sand and crush it with his heel. He stood like an old gunslinger, peerin at the old house. The bottom of his cassock was ripplin in the evenin seabreeze. I got out the car to join him and Rico followed me, but only because he didn't want to be left alone. 'It's a nice evenin,' Father Anton say, still lookin at the house. 'You know, you two are lucky. Some people go their entire lives never seeing the ocean.'

Father Anton sat on a log and motion for us to go in the water. But we wasn't feelin to bathe. He say to us, 'We've come all this way. Go ahead – the water is yours.'

Rico look at me and then back at Father Anton. Then at the ocean. His eyes linger on it for a minute or so. He then pull his shirt over his head, pouting his lips like it was a chore. I did the same. We gave our clothes to Father Anton and he kept them on his lap. In just our underwear, we marched to the water. And under the sunset, we waded round in waxmelt-gold.

He sat quietly with the cigarette in his hand and watched us. Me and Rico didn't say a word to each other. We didn't even bathe next to each other. He was hobbling through the water slow and clumsy like an overgrown lobster, letting each wave clobber him right in the face. His eyes was red.

But it coulda just been the salt.

When we got back, Sister Kitty was gone. Guitar and songbook and all. Sister Mother and Father Anton didn't say nothin about anythin, where she went, what was the next step for her, but that didn't change a damn thing. Everybody know what she did. I never find out for sure what had become of her. But no charges was ever filed. And, like Father Anton proclaim, no headlines was ever made.

The choir still went on, but the music wasn't the same. Not without the guitar. Father Anton find someone who coulda play the keyboard. Sister Mother sat in on rehearsal from then on. The songs didn't change. The Sunday people ask for Kitty every once in a while and all Father Anton coulda reply was, 'Moved onto other pastures.' But none of us never really spoke bout her again. If they did, she was referred to by her real name, Sister Katherine Ines Lewis.

But never in fond memory.

I drew stares from the other children for a while. They didn't stare me down. No, just the opposite. Their eyes hovered over me when I wasn't payin attention. Rey would look at the floor anytime I came close. Jeannine would start fiddlin with her hair. Sookie had a funny way of hidin her discomfort. She'd pretend like a mosquito just bit her arm. The whole thing was a coordinated system to shove me into the corner of their eyes.

My presence in a room could slow the clocks. The very sound of my name would rotate necks and turn eyes upward, downward, sideways. They was strange to Rico too. Quenton and Rico didn't talk much after that.

Ti-Marie wasn't the same either. She seem to lose her voice when she was around me. Her shoulders would slump, her lips would shrivel, she would have trouble swallowing. One night, she come into my room and wrap her arms round me like an octopus. When she was done, the front of my jersey was soaked with tears.

I'm not sure if it actually happen, though. I always feel like I took it from a dream.

7

'I will come and fuck them up!'

★

I remember the day Elroy disappear from St. Asteria. He went to bed on Divali night and wasn't nowhere to be seen come mornin. Yes, in the Festival of Lights, he disappeared in the darkness. Dogs, too, was known to go missin after Divali – the firecrackers would trip them off.

We was all shaken awake with interrogations by Sister Mother, askin if we knew his whereabouts. Nobody knew shit. Elroy roomed by himself, so there was no witnesses. Sister Mother gather us in the dining room and began recallin the facts.

Everyone was back in their rooms after Father Anton's fireworks display. Everyone was clappin and shriekin at the bottle rockets and bamboo bangers – everybody except Elroy. Father Anton give us all a deya, with some oil and a cotton wick. He worship the Christian God, yes, but he also had faith in the gods of his fellow men. Ti-Marie lit my deya for me, and I lit hers. We spelt our names in the air with sparklers and chased each other round with *Fun Snaps*. I grabbed a handful of snaps and flung them in the air. Then everybody started doin it. 'America droppin bombs! Look out!' Ti-Marie yell out. Tiny raindrops of fire, noise and sawdust pelt down on the street. As we tried not to get hit, we shove each other into the blitzkrieg. It was the first time I find myself laughing with everyone in a long time.

Elroy sat near the drain by himself, face like a puffer fish. Quenton say he wake up bout three in the mornin to pee and Elroy was still in bed. This was valuable information for the authorities. They give him what they call a four-hour window. This country is damn small too. Where you coulda really reach in four hours? They was fairly certain they coulda recover the boy. But judging from their tone, I know they wasn't goin to try too hard.

Father Anton drive round for bout two or three hours daily. Elroy's bulk woulda make him not hard to miss, but there was no trace of the boy. Vanish like a fart in the wind.

While they was concerned bout findin Elroy, I was more curious bout how he got out. Locked front door. Windows was shut. He was too fat to scale the wall and the gate outside. Couldn't tunnel underneath. So, how did he do it? Flush himself down the toilet? If he manage to pry the window open, how did it lock itself after he climb out? Somebody had to help him. But nobody had a fuckin clue. Nobody knew Elroy, nor cared to. Nobody never bother Elroy and Elroy never bother nobody.

I had the feelin that he didn't escape – that maybe somebody kill his ass and stick him beneath the floorboards, or in some hidden wall or cupboard, and that if I was to go right now and look hard enough, I'd find a wide-ribbed skeleton with rat-bit greying flesh slippin from the bones somewhere in one of the cubbyholes.

I revisit that Divali night sometimes. Mightn't sound like much to other people, but it was real happiness. It was special because it was a reminder of how you could revel in a moment, as fleeting as it is, cut off from everyday misery. It was one of them moments other moments coulda be measured by. See, round this time, me, Rey, Rico and Quenton get placed in secondary schools. Four different ones, so we was all strangers in a strange land. Secondary school was enough to crush you into dust – it was nothin but time and pressure. Now that we was there, though, we felt big. And the girls felt big, too, just by bein close to us. This wasn't necessarily a good thing. Big ain't the same as strong. It just mean that you was an easier target – easier to be scoped out and locked on.

Rico didn't take well to secondary school. He met a new breed of bad there. By the end of September, not even a month in, he was comin home with bruises, black eyes and a battered ego. He stay in his room most of the time. Maybe he was too shame to show his face round everyone cause of that. God forbid if Rico woulda let us see him bleed. In October, they suspend him for carryin an icepick to school.

Rey didn't hang with nobody much anymore either. All he was interested in was business, as he call it. His school only use to sell them local snacks. You know, salt prunes, preserved mangoes and rainbow-dyed sugar plums. Rey aimed to give them competition. He use to buy them American snacks from the kiosks round the neighbourhood that the stalls in school didn't sell. M&M's, Skittles, them Willy Wonka candies. He'd carry them round in a separate red bookbag. He was a big hit in school, could tell you that.

Anyway, we was in the study, sittin cross-legged on the carpet, playin All Fours. Well, they was playin – Ti-Marie, Sookie, Quenton and Jeannine – I was trying to finish a book report for a teacher who never used to bother come to class.

The girls got to talkin bout Elroy.

'I don't understand why that boy wanted to run away,' Ti-Marie say.

'He was a weird boy, you know,' Sookie add.

'Girl,' Jeannine say. 'You know what sad? I never really get to talk to him. The boy was just a stranger.'

Sookie cut in, 'He never used to talk to anybody, girl, so don't beat yourself up. Some people just like to live like that.'

'You ain't know you have to watch out for the quiet ones?' Quenton say, laughing, finally dropping a card to make his play.

'True talk,' Ti-Marie say.

Sookie turn to me. 'Jordon, you ever talk to him?'

'Once or twice. But it wasn't bout nothin, really.'

Jeannine play a card and say, 'You lucky, boy. I once had that boy for the Christmas gift exchange. The boy didn't even tell me Merry Christmas.'

'What you buy for him?' Quenton asked.

'Perfume.'

Quenton laughed. 'I wouldn't tell you Merry Christmas either. I know I does smell bad, but that is some rude shit, bitch.'

'Oh gosh, Quenton, boy, that *word*,' Ti-Marie say, tamping her thumbs in her ears.

'Bitch bitch bitch bitch bitch,' Quenton mutter.

Sookie play her hand and ask, 'You all think he would come back?'

'Why he ain't gon come back?' Ti-Marie say. 'He stupid? What he gon eat? Where he gon sleep? Where he gon do his business? Reality goin to catch up just now and he gon come back. Wait and see.'

'Sista, I know stupid,' Quenton say, 'and when I use to look at that boy, I ain't never call he stupid. He take the leap, but he ain't do it without workin it out in he head first.'

Ti-Marie ask, 'What you gon call him then?'

Quenton was fannin his chin with his cards. Then he say, '*Clear-voyered*. That is the word, right? That is how you does say it, right?'

'Clairvo*yant*,' I say, raising my head from the book report.

Quenton say, 'My nigga. *Clairvoyant*, yeah. The boy know he future already. You bitches ever think bout what you goin to be after you done with St. Asteria? Eh? None of we here gon end up livin in palaces, you know.'

'Unless I marry you, Quenton,' Jeannine say, and the girls laugh.

Quenton say, 'Yeah, easy for a girl to say. Gold diggin is a female profession. Elroy know he wasn't goin to be nothin once he spend the rest of his days in here. Fat boy wanted to give heself a head start in life.'

'And what bout you, Mr. Quenton?' Sookie ask. 'Why you don't give yourself a nice big head-start in life?'

'Listen, bitch, I ain't ready to be eatin outta no fuckin rubbish bin.'

Ti-Marie cut in, 'Your mouth is the rubbish bin!'

Jeannine sighed. 'You can't be serious. You sayin somebody who thinkin straight gon look to run away from their home and become a stray dog, Quenton?'

Quenton shrug. 'Nigga, it is what it is. All of you who does call this place *home*. This is not your home. Sister Mother not your mother. Father Anton not your father. Your mother and father either dead or lost.'

'Shut up, Quenton,' Ti-Marie say. 'They take the time to raise everybody here. They good people.'

'I say they's bad people, sista? Listen for once in your life, and stop backtalkin. They's just humans. It only have so much they could do.'

Jeannine say, 'Even if that is the case, I still ain't see how somebody gon want to cut short the little time they have here. Nobody does just wake up and decide to be a stray.'

'First smart thing you say today,' Quenton say. 'Nobody decide to be a stray.'

'Then explain yourself,' Ti-Marie say.

'You know what they does say bout elephants?'

Sookie say, 'Good memory?'

Quenton shake his head. 'No. Bout when it is their time to die.'

I cut in. 'They march to their graves.'

'You gon grow up to be somethin great, Sant.' Quenton start clappin. 'Elephants know when they goin to die. They wait till a while before and then they start the march. The march of death. But they don't stray from the herd till a short while before.'

'What is your point, Quenton?' Jeannine ask.

'Elroy the elephant,' Quenton say with a smirk, 'march to his grave.'

'God, Quenton,' Sookie say. 'I can't wait till you do the same.'

'Listen, bitches, what you think the first day of secondary school is like?'

'We gon find that out next year,' Ti-Marie say, 'but not too different. Is all the same. Teachers. Books. Only the place and people is different.'

Quenton laugh. Honestly, I ain't blame him for laughin. Sometimes I wanted to drink bleach just so I didn't have to go to school.

I tell them, 'There should be a religion that prepare you for secondary school. The first day you walk in, you ain't among children no more. Everybody is husband and wife suddenly. Everybody ready to fight. And nobody willin to stop it.'

Quenton continue, 'You girls might be the Three Musketeers now, but when the time come to move on from St. Asteria, you really think you bitches have it in you to keep it together? People become strangers real fast.'

Their eyes flitted to each other, trying to hide their frowns. Quenton's smile was wide. He say, 'Elroy know he was goin to have to say goodbye. I think that is why he never bother to talk to nobody. He know he was goin to have to get out there when the time come. He didn't want to wait for that.'

The three girls was still silent. Quenton continue, 'Eighteen is too late to start learnin to be a stray dog. It have nothin like a new

74

stray. Dogs with old tricks useless in the street. A runaway dog don't become a stray until it learn to survive. See, you's either born a stray or you suffer to earn the title.'

'I just glad you gon be marchin off before anybody else here.' Jeannine storm off, flinging away her cards in disgust.

'Why she mad?' Quenton ask the other girls.

But the other girls just follow suit.

What Quenton say bout learning to be a stray make more and more sense. Had a man who live cross the road, near the old park. Mr. Granger, a drunk old goat who couldn't feel no connection to the world unless he was beatin his wife. Heard he was worse when he was sober. The kinda man who only had a drinkin problem when he couldn't get a drink. The whole street coulda hear the screams of the Missus on some nights.

Sister Mother had to call the police on him a couple times. Probably save Mrs. Granger's life some of them nights – not that it ever mean anythin to the woman. She never press charges on him. In fact, she woulda ask why Sister Mother didn't mind her own damn business. She always claim it was her own fault for making her husband go mad. Didn't put enough salt in the broth. Put too much pepper in the stew. Didn't remember to wash the dishes. All major felonies in the Granger household. The more shit Granger was allow to do, the more I understand why Sister Mother felt the way she did bout the place. This was the Trinidad that surrounded Sister Mother. We was taught to tolerate Trinidad, not love it.

Well, round this time, Granger get himself a dog – a fuzzy little Rott, small like a Christmas ornament. But it had a big dog name – Chopper. Chopper was always pouncin and prancin on the dirt, takin chase after lizards and pigeons. But the dog wasn't allowed to be happy. Nothin was allowed to be happy in the Granger residence. I tell you, Granger fuck that dog up. He use to pay them ratty little schoolboys to come to his yard and beat the dog with an old steel pipe. Five dollars a session. Swear some of them boys woulda do it for free. Beat the heart and soul right outta that dog. The reason? 'To make it bad,' he say. Had no police we could call for this one. A dead dog is nobody else business – what you gon do to prevent it? That was the man's property.

We learn never to walk on that side of the road after witnessing what Granger was doin to that dog – and Granger never like children anyway, especially since his own never want anythin to do with him.

The dog look at me once when I was walkin home from school, my head still rattlin from gettin slam against the wall, my arm bruised. I was feelin to cry. I was this dog, I tellin you. Its eyes big and brown, sulkin in the sun, chain to an old post, scramblin for shade under a thorny midden of cast-iron and bicycle parts. Ashamed of its mange, retreating from every face that pass front the house.

See, I make the mistake of steppin on a pair of shoes. Wasn't just any shoes. These shoes had belong to Bronson Bailey. Bronson the Bastard Badjohn Bailey, who come to school with his shirt outside his pants and load up on bayrum and Vincey, and not one man jack coulda tell him shit bout it. Whenever he pass through the halls, everybody had to clear the way unless they wanted to end up pile on top of a flesh slagheap. You and all your friends. See, the misery of the world is cause by boys like Bailey – boys with small hearts who had to raise hell to feel big.

Steppin on Bronson's shoe was a moment that change my life. Life was a constant volcanic eruption after that. I was treadin on lava. I was scared, tell you, scared for my life. I used to beg Sister Mother to stay home. I never wanted to let her know the extent of the nightmare. It was shameful. I didn't want nobody to know. I try my best to hide the bruises. Once they wasn't on my face, I didn't have to worry. I remember seein how Rico was, comin home. Couldn't take it. That was why he carry the ice-pick to school that time.

Even though I do what I do to Kitty, Rico let bygones be bygones. Bein out there in the wild make him realize how little the problems in St. Asteria was. Holdin on to anythin else was impossible. Might as well let it go. I wouldn't say we respected each other, but we coulda walk round in each other's shoes for a bit.

'You was really gon stab him?' I ask Rico.

'Boy, I ain't know.'

'How you could not know? You think you had it in you?'

'Have it in me? What the fuck that mean, have it in me?'

76

'You don't feel you coulda do it?'

'Hoss, push a man too far and he could do anything. It have shit you don't want to know you could do. You mightn't think you capable right up to the point you actually fuck a man up.'

'But you didn't do nothin.'

'Look. Even if you land a blade in a man skull, we ain't have it in we to deal with what come after. We ain't bad like some of them out there, boy. Them is a different breed. We have to stay far from bein like that. Tell you, always have somebody worse than you, boy. Ain't make sense to be bad if you ain't the worst. If you ain't learn that, and learn that fast, start diggin your grave.'

So when he went back to school, he learn to take his beatings and shut his mouth. He claim he was better off that way.

God would get me through this. God would give me the strength. Through the beatings, I pray. As much as I try to rationalize it, I couldn't. All because of a fuckin shoe? Beating after beating. It was the loneliest thing in the world, gettin shoved to the ground and have three people kick you in the balls. It was hell. Couldn't depend on nobody. Wasn't like when all of us in St. Asteria was under the same roof.

You'd look up and see the crowd of spectators through your tears. Most of them would be cheerin. Sometimes people just need to see things bleed. I guess silence was the scariest thing in the world for some of these children – louder than the shouts and the cackles.

Bronson was in the papers that month. Not by name – he was too young. He was still in Form Five. He and his minions stone one of the teachers in the car park. She know it was them, but she didn't want to name them to the police. 'If she say anything, is mi brethren up by me gon do for she,' Bronson say. 'A black car gon roll up and that is the last sight she gon see!' The Principal just pretend the boy ain't exist. Even the security guards used to fraid him. People work too damn hard to have some shit-head child snuff their life outta them. He was gon be outta their hands in a year, anyway. Let the streets take care of him – let a creature like that die its natural death.

Couldn't call in no parents for no conference because he didn't live with his parents. He live with his girlfriend's family somewhere in Princes Town and, from what I hear, they didn't want him round neither, but they couldn't tell him nothin. Not even the girlfriend wanted anythin to do with him, but he make sure he coulda still come and go as he please, and take whatever he want, including the girl's body. I imagined her moans echoing for the whole rickety house to hear, the parents hiding under their cover in the next room, biting their nails, waitin for the screak-screak-screak of the bed to come to a stop.

One day, Quenton saw one of the bruises on my arm. He pull me aside in his room, a serious look on his face – in fact, I never see him so serious before. A fatherly kinda serious. 'Which dog-fucker do that to you?' he ask me, lifting the bill of his cap.

I kept watchin the floor. I didn't want to talk, but he was determined. He say, 'Have nobody in here lookin out for none of we. You understand? We have to take care of we own.'

'I ain't lookin for trouble.'

'Fuck you, Gandhi. You ain't have to look for trouble, bitch. Trouble lookin for people like we all the time. You ain't know that? We have to band together if we want to survive. You take licks once like is nothin? Might as well take it your whole life, young'n.'

'I understand.'

'I ain't think you understand shit.'

'I ain't want to make things worse, Quenton.'

'Things ain't waitin for you to make it worse! See, you ain't fuckin understandin me, young'n. Have a reason I startin to run things in my school, you know. You have to be fearless. Now is the time to decide how you want your life to go down.'

'I could take care of myself.'

He suck his teeth. 'When you ready, drop a name. I will come and fuck them up!'

I didn't have nothin to say to that. Quenton had that hot blood flowin through him. Truces mean nothin to him. He was a soldier now. A hitman for hire, it seem. I suppose goin to a war-zone everyday will do that to you. I couldn't go that route. I couldn't believe in livin like that.

Have a hierarchy in this universe. People talk bout heaven being in the skies and hell underground. I don't believe that. Ain't no way you gon have people willin to climb downwards. Nobody gon jump down no hole like that. No, here we have two ladders, equally tall, equally strong. One branded law and one branded chaos. Everybody wanna reach the top, by hook or by crook. Once you start climbin, either keep climbin or fall.

This is a long road that has no turning, right?

8

'Easy way to kill somebody who already killin theyself.'

★

Close to Christmas, a year after Mouse left, a French Creole girl, Marissa Kelly, got ship over to St. Asteria. But everyone just call her Pinky. She had dark brown curls, green eyes, and unlike the other girls, had already filled out.

Pinky soon let us know how she end up in St. Asteria. Apparently her father abandon her, bib still round her neck, and hitch a banana boat back to Guadeloupe, leaving Pinky with her small-time coke-dealer mother.

'Just a pawn who feel she was a queen,' Pinky use to say bout her mother. 'Knock off the board before she even realize.'

Pinky was bout fourteen when they jostle her ass in with us. She had a life from before. Not like how me and Rey and Ti-Marie was here since before we could remember. When she first come, we didn't really consider her part of the family. We wasn't even sure if she was goin to be permanent, or if she was just a passin cloud. No godparents was ever established, and authorities didn't try too hard to get in contact with her father, so nothin ever come of that. Nothin come of any attempt to reach out to the grandparents either. So, St. Asteria just decide to keep the damn girl.

She talk too damn much. First, she went on and on bout school. Then she try to pull us in to write her essays. Nobody paid attention. That was when the talk start up bout all the suitors her mother had. Hardback gangster men who tattoo verses on their chest, but exchange religion for code – men who only God can judge. Then she drop the bomb – how she lost her virginity to one of them. Well, from then, we was all ears.

She lose her virginity to a man who call himself Glass. She never know his real name. Her mother probably never did neither. She just say that one night he climb into bed with her and start doin it. She say how girls suppose to pretend like they can't stand it – that fellas like to hear that. But with Glass, wasn't no pretend. Pinky say his penis like a cutlass inside of her. She didn't like it. And she bleed out after. It was long and thick like her hand.

'Sheeit,' Quenton say. 'Mine bigger than that.'

Say she was twelve when it happened. Glass was in his late twenties. Glass and her mother had a big fight the next night and he smack her in the eye so hard, it swell up for two weeks.

When we got bored of Glass, she start talkin about Damon, her mother's next boyfriend. Younger than the last one, bout twenty or so. She say even though Glass took her virginity, her first kiss was with Damon.

Say how she was in her room, lyin on the carpet with the radio on. He come in and he look tall like a moko jumbie. Say how he tell her to sit on the bed. Then he kneel in front of her and he cupped her chin, tenderly strokin the corners of her lips with his fingers. She talk bout how fast her heart was beatin, much faster than with Glass. 'Then he move in slow and kiss me, and my body tremble. I get wet, wet, wet.'

She use to feel special round him – couldn't get enough. He use to *make love* to her and treat her like a woman. Before they made love, he would put on a slow jam and hold her tight against his naked body. 'Was a different level of fuckin, a whole new world.'

'So, how your mother ain't find out?' Rey ask.

'I think the bitch had know. She use to fall asleep – bam! – right after a hit, and that was when me and the man use to do we business. A couple times she wake up in the middle of it, mutterin some nonsense. She probably convince sheself that she was hallucinatin. Damon didn't come over to see she. He come to see me. That is why he use to bring the bag of coke every time. To get the bitch high and outta she mind. Outta the picture.'

'You didn't feel bad?' Rey ask.

'Bad, why? Feel good to be wanted.'

'You use to love the lovin, eh?' Quenton did say.

'The only man I ever love.'

'You tell him that?' Quenton ask.

Pinky suck her teeth. 'Me lovin him is none of he damn business.'

Quenton raise his eyebrows and grin. Ti-Marie, who was just sitting in the corner, shook her head. Couldn't take no more. As she left the room, she say, 'I don't agree with this at all.'

Pinky talk bout the time her mother come home minutes to mornin and fall face-down on the ground. 'Like a bag of bricks.' A tattered dress, slippin halfway down her shoulder and hikin halfway up her thighs with blood smeared on their insides. She wasn't wearin no panties neither, but the blood didn't look like it come from her vagina. It was from a stab wound somewhere on the inner thighs. A trickle of dried blood was pasted over her forehead and her jaw was shifted to the side. Her eyes was demon-red. 'She eyes just kinda roll to the back of she head. But she was tryin to look at me at the same time.'

In the emergency room, the doctors say she had a fractured jaw, two broken ribs, a burn on her arm, minor haemorrhaging and that she had tears in her vaginal wall. She was also sky-high on coke. In the police statement, she say she get into a taxi and the driver take her into the middle of a field where he and some men beat her senseless. She musta pass out during the rape. But Pinky didn't believe this, nor the police neither. 'Them didn't even bother to ask how she reach home after that,' Pinky say.

Pinky was put in a home for a couple of months before her mother recovered and reclaimed her. She tell us bout how she fuck two of the boys in there – one in the closet and one in the bathroom – but that it wasn't the same. Pinky say she was ravin mad that time because she couldn't see Damon no more. She think that Damon was one of the men who raped her mother.

Pinky and her mother then got placed in a new housing project near Arima. But her mother didn't take long to fall back into her old bad habits. This time, instead of passin out when she take a hit, she'd get to apologizing.

'Bitch would just be tellin me how she sorry,' Pinky say. 'Bout a hundred times a day. Sayin how she sorry, how she so *sorry*. She didn't know she coulda do she baby like that. It was real sickenin, havin somebody tell you so much that they sorry. I ain't want nobody feelin sorry for me.'

But that wasn't the end. Pinky's next story was bout the time *she* had to go to the hospital. 'Had this rasta I had my eyes on,' she say. 'He live up the road by me. He was a young buck, bout twenty, and livin by heself. He face was always under a car hood. He didn't have no education or nothin, but people use to say the man was a wizard with cars. They use to call him Fix. We start talkin one day, and he get to askin bout my mother and if the hospital treat she right. But I change the topic quick. I tell him he have a nice body. The whole time I givin him the eye and the swagger but you coulda swear the fella was a batty-boy, because he wasn't havin none of it.'

Quenton was strokin his chin. 'Rasta have morals, you know.'

Pinky continue, 'So one day, I make Fix take me inside and I jump 'im. He fall backwards on the couch, and I grab him by he big balls and start kissin 'im. He start mumblin something but I wasn't listenin. Then he start kickin me round. Man went mad. He throw me off and start kickin me in the ribs. All the while, he bawlin, *You gon put me in jail, you gon put me in jail!'*

'Fuckin madman,' Quenton say.

'That man was mentally unsound, boy! He pick me up and pelt me cross the room. He was still yellin, but I couldn't understand nothin. He was dribblin all over. I was breathin hard, watchin this crazy asshole lash he arms all over, knockin over everything in the house. Mashin up he own damn house! Then he grab a pack of cigarette and bolt out the door.'

'And?' I prodded.

'They lock him up. I ain't know where he is now. But he lock up somewhere, I hope. I was in the hospital for bout two weeks. He crack two of my fuckin ribs, yes. That shit hurt like hell.'

Pinky say how her mother fly into a frenzy when she hear the news. 'The bitch just come home and start sharin out licks. She finally realize that I wasn't no victim. As soon as she reach home, she take off she belt and start whippin away at everything. Sometimes two belt at once. But she get a new boyfriend soon enough. This one use to call heself Powers. He was a big one, look like he coulda cuff holes in the wall.'

'I could do more than that,' Quenton say, flexing his arm.

Pinky say, 'And my mother pull me aside one day in the

kitchen and slap me and tell me not to go round this one – how this is she own.'

'Did you?' I ask.

'Aye, you feel she could stop me?' Pinky say. Everybody laughed. 'But it wasn't my idea. I ain't so devious one time. He was playin Damon game but with different rules. Bring coke anytime he come over. But not as a distraction. Payment. She could get a couple hits by pimpin me out, she realize. I never wanted to do nothin with him, though. He frighten me. She never let him fuck me, though. Just other things. I remember the first time she ask me to do it – bitch was high as a fuckin kite. She say, *Pinky, do this for mommy, okay? It not takin much outta you. You ain't have to swallow.*'

'Bet you swallow, anyway,' Quenton say.

Pinky say, 'It went like that for bout a month. Until she start to cause trouble and start goin to the police. That is when Powers give she the hot shot.'

'Hot shot?' Quenton ask.

'He put somethin in the batch,' she say. 'Easy way to kill somebody who already killin theyself. So she take the bait. Shoot up straight in she arm with the glass gun. Poison racing through she blood. I remember how she went mad for a minute or two before gravity hit she. Before she hit the ground, she give me the same kinda look the nights she was in the hospital. Eyes rollin back but lookin like she strainin to look at me at the same time.'

'And what happen after?' I ask.

'She mouth was frothin with blood and she was floppin bout like a damn fish,' Pinky say. 'Then after bout ten-twenty seconds, she stop. And that was it, boys. Murder she wrote.'

Pinky disrupted the natural order of things. She'd sneak out of the girls hall and come in the boys hall. Didn't have no set of sneakin to do, but nobody else ever did that – not even Rico and Quenton. Pinky just came and throw everythin up in the air, went wherever she damn pleased.

I remember the first time I saw her in the boys hall. Was in Rico and Quenton's room. Rico wanted no part of it. Quenton was on the floor with his pants down to his knees and she was kneelin on top of his crotch with only a white bra on. She was gigglin quietly as she was bouncin up and down. Quenton was bareback, biting his bottom lip and runnin a palm along her chest, pinchin her nipples.

Rey was sittin on the bottom bunk, just watchin. I remember bein surprised at how quiet they was. Like they was watchin the TV on mute.

Pinky spun round to look at me. Even with her jaw hangin open like a Venus flytrap, the smirk was apparent. Cheeks flushed with clammy redness. Then she pressed a hand down on Quenton, grabbin his chest hair as if it would help her balance, and pursed her lips at me before blowin me a kiss.

'The fuck you all doin?' The words just push outta my mouth.

'The fuck you think we doin, Sant?' Quenton say, laughing.

'Unhook my bra, boy,' Pinky say to me, smiling still.

'Sant, you want a turn?' Quenton ask.

'Sant ain't gon do shit,' Rey say, not even watchin me.

'Fuck you.' My first words to him in a long time,

Rey got up and did it himself. He pushed the right cup of the bra against his nose, makin him look like a demented surgeon.

Meantime, Pinky was doin a 180 on Quenton to face me. She grabbed her tiny breasts and pushed them together, still bobbin up and down.

'Gimme a kiss, boy,' she say, puckerin her lips at me.

'No,' I say.

'Why?' She made a pretend sad-face.

'Don't want to.'

'Faggot,' Rey say. 'Don't worry, baby,' he say, gettin up from the bed, 'Look a kiss.' He knelt at her side and nudged her face to the side with one finger. Their lips didn't even touch at first, he just plunged his tongue into her mouth.

'Ooh. Everybody so friendly here, boy. This my new favourite place.'

I went back to bed.

This became a staple of the boys' hall. Pinky ridin Quenton, and Rey touchin himself through his pants. Every night. Sometimes I'd peep from the doorway. The boys never noticed me but Pinky use to know, because the next day, she'd come close and whisper in my ear, 'How the peepin was?'

'Nasty bunch of boys,' Ti-Marie say. 'Jordon, you make yourself a part of that?'

'I don't bother nobody. And nobody don't bother me,' I told her. 'That is them business.'

'I gon tell on all of you one of these days,' Jeannine snap, soundin much more upset than I had expect from her.

'Boys just filthy on a whole,' Ti-Marie say.

'The people didn't come give you all the AIDS talk in school yet or what?' Jeannine say. 'I ain't gon be surprised to find out that lil jammette bring disease up in here.'

'I ain't want to talk bout it,' I say. 'Talk to them, not me, if all of you feelin so bothered by it. I ain't like she either, you know. But is really not my business.'

Sometime during the next couple days, I noticed something weird when Pinky was comin outta the bathroom. Under the white towel wrapped round her body, a red line ran down the side, blottin around her hip. When I went to use the bathroom after, I saw a razorblade with a speckle of blood on it. She was cuttin herself. During the next romp, I went to see if I coulda pinpoint the wound.

The first thing I see was Quenton sittin on the bed and Pinky bobbin up and down. She and Rey was doin it. That come as a big shock to me, that one make me feel sick. Still does.

I didn't say nothin. I just left. Whenever I saw Rey from then on, I felt like a worm squirmin up from my throat. That moment made me realize how far gone everything was, how everything get so fucked in St. Asteria. But for how long had the floor been missin under my feet? Was like in them cartoons where they run straight off the cliff but don't fall unless they look down. Now I was lookin down and there was nothin beneath me.

You realize your life has been a long scream, and now there's no voice left. Guess that's why Sister Mother once say that the world ends not with a bang, but with a whimper. Probably there gon be a moment when God get fed up of us. He'll put out the sun and leave us frozen. That's the whimper she talk bout. Why hold on? Why stay and watch everythin round you wither and die?

When you get to this point, anythin goes. Your actions ain't summin up for no long-term goal. So when I slammed Bronson's head against a pole and emptied a garbage bin over his head the next day, all I was interested in was how people would react – which ain't much considerin the thin line I was walkin between life and death. Well, that moment, time stopped. Everyone round me was dead silent. A janitor in the distance drop his cigarette. The badjohn under me writhed between my feet, his uniform splashed with juice and dribs of soda. A halo of flies already gather round him.

They didn't have to take me to the Principal's office. I went willingly and admitted my crimes. They suspended me. One week! I was disappointed. I was lookin forward to expulsion. I think it was mostly to protect my ass. They give me one extra week to live, if that. But when I got back to St. Asteria to deliver the news, Sister Mother was furious. Seem she believe the attack come out of nowhere.

She ain't care. Nobody wanted to hear nothin. They didn't want to see Jordon, the beaten dog. They wanted to see Jordon, the rabid beast. 'You don't answer violence with violence!' Sister Mother keep sayin over and over. I keep my mouth clamp shut, because if I had open it I was goin to cuss. She wanted me to break bread with Bronson? Turn the other cheek? I wanted to spit out, *If I answer with anything else, is death for me!* She want me to wait for him to fuckin chop me up and feed me to his dog?

Father Anton call me to the pews one evenin. He send Ti-Marie to get me from my room. While we was walkin to the parish, she ask me, 'You really beat him up?'

I hesitated. 'Why you ask?'

'Rico get to stay home, too, but he didn't beat up nobody.'

'Yeah. I beat him up.'

'He probably had it comin then.'

I nodded. 'You could say so.'

'I think you had to do what you had to do,' she say. 'Else you wouldn't have done it.'

Truth was that the whole situation wasn't no big moral conundrum for me. Who give a fuck bout right and wrong when you're bein kick down to the ground?

'Why you think he does it?'

'Who?'

'The boy you beat up. Why you think he cause trouble for you?'

I shrug. 'That's just how he is.'

'You think so?'

'If he ain't doin what he doin, he don't feel like himself, I guessin.'

'I hope it don't have nobody like that when I start secondary.' She look me in the eye. 'You think you goin to drop outta school?'

I laugh. 'I wish.'

'Remember when you tell me you had nothin to offer?'

'Yeah.'

'You still think that is true?'

'I dunno.'

Ti-Marie sit on the steps outside the church. I scoot next to her. She put my hand in hers. 'You know how Quenton was talkin,' she say, 'how all of we gon drift apart.'

'Yeah.'

'I don't want that to happen.'

'It might.'

She let go of my hand and cradle her chin against my shoulder, her lips against my neck. 'I think we have to work to let that not happen. All of we here, we's family.'

'Our families are gone.'

'Family ain't who blood in you, you know. Family is who you choose to be with.'

Mouse immediately shoot to mind. I pry Ti-Marie off me and say, 'Till they choose to go away.'

Ti-Marie call out to me, but I was already in the church.

Father Anton sit next to me, leanin forward, his fingers steepled against his chin. He watch me for a long time before speakin. 'Have you been reading your Bible lately, Jordon?'

'The Bible isn't going to help me in that school, Father.'

'And you think your fists would help?' He waved his knuckles around. 'You think there's more influence in these? You think your life is better now that you've used these?'

'Father, you don't understand –'

'I understand that evil is something you bring unto yourself.'

When he said that, I was pissed off. I did *not* invite Bronson into my life. I did not bring my current situation unto myself. But then Father Anton added, 'I'm not saying you asked for this. But you certainly did not make your life better by doing what you did.'

'What can I do then?'

'You need to apologize. Be the bigger man.'

My blood crawl when he say that, but I wasn't gon fight him.

'You know why Jesus said the meek would inherit the earth, Jordon?'

'No.'

'You ever heard about the space race?'

I shook my head. He continued, 'Between the Americans and the Russians. When the Americans started sending astronauts up to space, they found out that their pens wouldn't work. Because there wasn't any gravity up there. The ink wouldn't flow down. So they had to develop a pen that would work in zero-gravity. They spent millions on this pen. But the Russians didn't have that kind of money. But they didn't need it. Do you know why?'

'Why?'

'The Russians used a pencil.' He chuckled. 'That's innovation.'

'So the Russians is the meek?'

He chuckled again. 'I wouldn't call the Russians meek in any way, but in this story, yes, they are.'

'This is a true story?'

'So I've heard. But do you know how it relates to what I'm saying?'

'The Russians was forced to make do.'

'Absolutely. The meek are trained through life to overcome any obstacle. And that's why they're the first ones in line to the Kingdom of Heaven.'

I nodded. 'First in line.' But what was really goin through my mind was were the Russian astronauts really first in line to get into the Kingdom of Heaven? If not, then shit, the meek is first in line to get into the Kingdom of Heaven because they's the first ones to be killed! Stayin where I was woulda be suicide. The Kingdom of Heaven could wait.

So on the day my suspension was up, I left to go to school and never arrive. And I didn't go back home. I toss my bookbag in a drain, took a walk along the highway and never turn back. I suspect they all talked bout me for a while and then forgot bout me. Probably not sooner than Elroy, but I didn't think I leave such a big, lasting impression on anybody.

At times, I use to wonder if I miss anybody or not. Couldn't figure it out. I cried. Plenty, plenty. I ain't gon lie – it wasn't easy. I cried, though I didn't regret anything. I know, on that day, there was nothing left in St. Asteria for me. What was happenin here wasn't no science experiment. *This was real*. It's them three words that echo through your mind when you make a decision like that. *This is real*.

History ain't no science experiment. There ain't nothin we could set up to make comparisons between different trials. Have no way to know what could be different. Can't go down two roads at once. Can't split our lives in two. We only have the one road. We choose that road and we don't stop.

II:

THE SINNERS

9

'Place like this – the house does always win.'

★

I followed the highway straight up to the capital. I started off hangin round the national library because I had nowhere else to go. You had to try to look like you wasn't hungry and homeless to get in there, though. But I had an advantage – I was young. Denying any youthman a chance to spend some time with books just seem wrong to most of the front security. I'd wait round till closing and hide in this recess at the bottom of the stairwell. Was always quiet down there, always felt clean, never cold, never infested with rats or anythin like that.

I was sleepy most of the time – like I was under a spell. The streets of Port-of-Spain could do that to you. All that carbon monoxide – you know, them colourless, odourless vapours that could sink you into a deep sleep. As I look back, sometimes I feel like I take half of it from dreams. If there was ever a time I rest my head on bare concrete, it wasn't for long. That wasn't the life for me. Couldn't stand existin as a tangle of limbs against a pavement edge, or a ragged shadow behind a streetlamp. I mean, I seen men like that all the time. But I always scrape to find ways to stay outta the cold. Whether I was bein shooed like a dog from the market; whether I was sprawl off amongst the poui petals on the savannah as people jogged over me, or driftin between the nonsense conversations while I roam the amber-lit promenade, I always know God was watchin over me. Had to believe it.

Had a small stretch near the lighthouse, where the air was thick like sweat, where the highway slimmed and intersected. I lived there for a while. I just stumble in and this man, who use to call himself Sanskrit, let me spend the night in his shack. When I ask him why he was being so kind, he just say, 'Don't tell me you ain't hear? Misery love company, pardner.'

He was slender, and he look like he was sculpted from shale. Grainy, flaky, uneven shale. Had a sunburnt beard mottled with the colour of tobacco. Grin begrimed with tar. Thick yellow nails. Eyes also yellow and blood-flecked. Always had a tattered cloth tied round his waist over a pair of ragged short pants. He was probably in his mid-thirties, but you can't be blame for mistakin him for fifty.

'The book say we should help out who we could,' he tell me, givin me a glass of water. 'But I think, in this case, we could help each other.' The bottom of the glass was caked with mud and a light murky film lined the crest of the water. But I still drink it. My throat was too parched to turn it down. We had salt crackers and guava jam for dinner. Candleflies was clickin on and off as they flit bout the room. The twisting trail of smoke from the mosquito coil let out a dull, fruity scent.

He gave me an old gasoline-stained bedsheet to cover myself with during the night. 'Now we in this together,' he say, drawin his sheet over his chin. Couldn't help noticin that his sheet was much cleaner than mine.

The shack was filthy. Seem like he didn't bother to throw nothin out. Mouldy bread on the corner of the counter, spiders creepin down from the ceiling, dust gatherin in the floor corners. He had a small fridge, but I ain't never see the point, because it ain't work. It was just another cupboard, and even that had been raided by maggots. Really make you question what kinda man could friend up with filth like this. I spent an entire week and clean the whole shack. Ain't needed nothin but a few pails of water and some blue soap. I exfoliated that shack, tellin you.

I barely sleep during the first few weeks. I constantly drifted in and out of dreams of St. Asteria, dreams of still bein there. I'd wake up, the pillow damp with sweat. It was hot in that shack. The sea was right there, but it wasn't the same one I see with Father Anton and Rico. This one was poisoned. During the day, when the tide recede, all you coulda see was muck on the shoreline. Sometimes you coulda see the dead fish. I knelt by the muddy water, my toes brushin against the overgrown weeds, and looked in the distance – a silhouette of forgotten ships just a half mile away.

Near the shack, there was a loop of rope tied round a metal beam bridgin two galvanize roofs. My first thought was that it was some kinda makeshift gallows. Maybe there was a story behind it and everybody make a pact to keep quiet bout it. I coulda imagine a body suspended from the rope, neck broken, toes pointin downwards, in slow rotations like meat on a rotisserie.

Live long enough in this galvanize wasteland and a man gon find it easy to believe there ain't no God. But had somethin I hear back in a sermon in St. Asteria, how you coulda become a victim of your own dirty mind, and whatever you put in your head makes its home there. So no matter how bad things get, I say, God watchin over me. Kept me alive when all voices round me was goin hoarse from screamin cusswords at wives and children.

They put sugar and starch in a pill and give it a fancy name. They give it to a dyin man and the next day death take one step back from him. Why? Because the man believe in the pill. Same way he believe in the pill, I believe in God.

In this muddy crust of a tidewrack place, collection of fishbones, political spraypaint on the patchwork of corrugated iron, you might take one look at these people and think that they is people that failed. I can see it in the faces of those who walk past, drive past. What's in there? Who livin there? Why bother?

But I took a walk one night to hear the steelpan harmonies from one of the houses. Up by the old dock, there was a young girl who like to sing. Never speak a word durin the day, but she had all manner of sad songs durin the night. The water mighta been teemin with shit, but if you see the crest at sunset, where the evenin sun spun like a wheel of light, for a moment you could see each strand of algae as the light knifed its way through the bubbling silt. I imagined Mouse was with me. Any fleeting moment of beauty, she was there.

I couldn't put myself above the people that live there. Somethin bout bein there made me feel I could start fresh. There wasn't no illusions, no lies. You had to find a spot where the light shine through and make it yours. Forget the boat graveyard. Forget the smell of shit that come with the rain. You do what you could to survive. You go out and find God in the fractures.

★

In the mornin, Sanskrit say, 'Today is Monday. And Monday is Dump Day. Get it straight.' He hand me a pair of oversized slippers and he grab an old baby pram from behind the shack. It was chained, like a dog to a steel pole, and covered with a small black tarpaulin. Sanskrit then introduce me to Greaves, a tall, lanky man with a beard like a billygoat, and a face long like one too. He didn't say or do much. He had a pickup. We pack the pram into the pickup and he take us to the nearby landfill.

A ring of black corbeaux was basking in the sun, having their fill of breakfast from the junk piles. 'Them not goin to do you nothin,' Sanskrit say. 'Them birds is my good neighbours.' He make a dash towards them, causing them to fly off.

'We lookin for non-ferrous metals,' Sanskrit tell me, runnin round and rummaging through the heaps. 'We pile it up in the pram here, and Greaves ship it off. He take a cut, I take a cut.'

'What bout me?'

'If you put in the right work, you gon get yours too. Right now, consider it an internship. Now get goin. Time is money. Non-ferrous metals only, eh, pardner.'

'Non-ferrous?'

'You ain't know what that mean? We lookin for brass, aluminium, nickel, copper. Copper pay sweet too bad.'

I gazed upon the stacks of galvanize, stoves and pipes. 'I sayin to you now, I dunno what is what.'

'Sheeit, you still new to the business. I gon learn you, don't worry.'

We filled that whole pickup with metal. I still couldn't tell what was what. I was hopin to God Sanskrit wasn't playin the metal specialist as a joke, because we was there for a good three hours after the sun come out blazin hot. 'Look up there,' he tell me, pointing to a flock of corbeaux orbiting the dump. 'Probably have a dead dog round there. What you say we grab it for lunch before them fellas up there get it, eh?'

I look at him like, *what the fuck!* He bust out laughin. 'Is jokes, boy! We gon eat good today and tomorrow with the money we making here. Tomorrow is Tuesday. Tuesdays we eat good. Thanksgiving. Write it down.'

When we got back, Sanskrit went out to get lunch. It didn't really have nothin to do but wait for him to return. Had this little girl who take an interest in me since I come to this town. Saw her gaze glued to me since the first time Sanskrit lead me in here. Couldn't be more than eight years old. She was by herself – I didn't know who her mother was, or which house she lived in.

'You ain't gone to school, boy?' she ask me, lining some glass bottles along an old table.

'Today not a school day,' I say.

'You feel this is the weekend?' She laughed and tapped some of the bottles with a spoon, producing a range of pitches.

'Monday is Dump Day,' I tell her.

She suck her teeth at me. I ask her, 'Why *you* ain't in school?'

'Ain't feel to go.'

'Why?'

She didn't give me an answer. She just went back to her bottles.

When Sanskrit come back, he had two styrofoam containers with him – barbecue chicken and fries from some town joint – and, in each of his pockets, two sweatin Heineken bottles. 'Lunch is served, me boy,' he say.

I tell him straight out, 'Don't buy no beer for me next time. Beer cost too much. I could just drink water. You could just gimme the money you woulda spend on it.

'You savin up for somethin, pardner?'

'You ain't need to buy food for me either. I could find my own. Just gimme the money you woulda spend on it.'

'My barbecue and fries not good enough for you, boss?'

'I could do with less and save the rest of the money.'

'You serious, boss? This petty cash you gon look to save up?' he say, taking a sip of the beer.

'Hadda start somewhere.'

'Well, fix your mix, boy-boy. You go on ahead and become a rich fella. Don't plan too much ahead, though, eh. Not here. Not in this place. Place like this – the house does always win. The wheel spins, the ball bounce however it want to bounce.'

'The ball?'

'You still young, pardner. You know how a smart man like me end up here?' He squint his eyes at the row of abandoned ships, smoothing the hairs at the nape of his neck. 'Risk, boy. Risk it all and lose. It don't pay to be a gamblin man. You know why?'

'Why?'

'Because no matter how the ball go or what hand you have or what horse you put down for, boy, the house does always win. The people up there think their shit is over when they flush the toilet. But is we down here who have to live in the sewers.' He turn to me. 'You understand what I sayin, pardner?'

'I think so.'

'Good. Tellin you, I am a scholar. A croupier. You must listen to me.'

And so, we had a schedule. A workin schedule. Monday was Dump Day. Tuesday was Thanksgiving, for Sanskrit, at least. I was busy saving my money while he drink himself silly. Wednesday was Emancipation Day. This was when Sanskrit free up himself with the Spanish girls at the local guest-house. 'A man have needs,' Sanskrit would say. I never had no interest to go with him. He never extend any invitations either.

Thursday and Friday was what he call the days of St. Vincent, named after Vincent de Paul, the patron saint of charity. Don't ask me how he know that shit – probably the man really was a scholar at some point. We use to just sit on the pavement near the bus stops and shake an old pan at passers-by. He say people was more likely to give money comin down to the end of the week. Told me not to try it on a Monday unless I was lookin for a good tongue-lashin.

'Pardner, you is a real money maker!' he tell me one day. He always went on how people was more likely to give to a beggar who either had a disability, a talent, or a dog with them. He didn't want to put on no shades and knock a broomstick all over the sidewalk, faking some blind man act. And he say he couldn't draw or sing for shit. So I was the advantage there. He wasn't gon toss me out and I wasn't goin nowhere. Before I come along, he used to take this stray dog named Sammy and walk it to town. A dog is like half a child, he say, counting his change. He didn't have no use for Sammy after his new dog, Jordon Sant, show up.

Friday night was the Baptism, where we wash the sins from our bodies and clothes. He tell me never to wash anything in the sea. The amount of shit and effluent they used to dump off there, I was surprised the fish didn't have three eyes. He never had no runnin water, but there was a couple of barrels and a bar of blue soap that we coulda use to wash ourselves and our clothes. We didn't keep close to anybody else, try our best never to bother nobody for nothin. Knowin people was trouble, Sanskrit say. You didn't want to end up with anybody who feel like you owe them. Not in this place.

Friday nights we had to clean ourselves because Saturdays was Christmas Eve, when we had to do all our shopping. Couldn't waltz in no supermarket lookin like a pair of smelly rats. Get thrown out. Mostly, we survive on a tin of salt crackers, hops bread, some butter or guava jam. We coulda make that last for days, boy.

And then Sunday was Christmas. Quiet, peaceful Christmas. All we had was a radio and a small TV, but we make do with it. At least it was in colour. Never miss an episode of *Family Matters* and *MacGyver*.

That was how the first four years pass. Four years is a long-ass time, but we had a routine and we make it work. Some people might call it madness to live comfortable in that manner. But as I say, God was in the fractures. You can think your way out of squalor, you know. At sixteen, shit, I was proud to have that talent. This was a whole new life. I never hungered for anything different. Not most of the time, anyway. Not that I didn't have ambition – I think I was just lackin imagination.

I only missed St. Asteria in my dreams. Time to time, I'd wake up rememberin the little shell frogs Mouse kept on her shelf. These was dead creatures. These was their coffins, collected from all different parts of the world. There wasn't no shells in the waters here. At least, I never see none. I'd wake up feelin flattened, trampled. All the world out there and I choose to live in this wasteland. But I only feel like that after the dreams. One minute later and I was back to normal. Sanskrit once tell me that dreams is wishes of the soul and nightmares is warnings for it. I suppose he had his share of them.

But even though I get back to normal, I couldn't ever get back to sleep. I'd sit by the boats and watch the sunrise over the city. The sun could give life to any brokedown carcass of a place, so I make it a habit to wake up and watch the sunrise. At the same time, the streetlights along the highway would dim.

It reminded me of the lamplighter chapter in *The Little Prince*, so I tell Sanskrit the story. 'You tellin me this man doin work and ain't gettin pay?' Sanskrit said.

'He just say orders is orders.'

'Well, pardner, that is how most people is. Seem like all this man waitin for is someone to come down from some office in God-knows-where and tell him that he get put off the payroll. People like this – slaves to the life they feel they have to live.'

'So what you's a slave to?'

'Me? I break way from all that. I's my own man. People with the best of morals is the biggest slaves. Most people waitin for a chance. They see the fruit in front of them but they fraid to pick.'

Eve and the apple immediately come to mind, but I didn't say nothin. He continued, 'Not sayin you ain't need morals. But if all you have in your life is your morals and nothin else, well, pardner, of what use is your life in the long run?'

★

I experience my first Carnival with Sanskrit. I remember sittin, most half asleep, at the topmost rung of the pavilion overlookin the bands. Clans of flabby, bareback men and scantily-clad women marchin slowly to the beat; a mosaic of colour and costume; everyone with a Stag in one hand, a cellphone in the other; rough legs scrapin against waxed thighs; backs brushin against chests; the wood beneath me vibratin with the music; soca so loud that you couldn't make out the lyrics.

Watched the people go by. A section of red people, then a section of purple people. Then a woman wearin a giant float on her back. Cloth, grass and beads, shimmerin under the blazin afternoon sun, spread like the wings of a deformed bird of paradise. Everything movin at the pace of dying earthworms.

But they keep marchin.

At St. Asteria we used to watch it on TV. That was the closest we ever get to it. Sister Mother believed that the idea behind

Carnival was an admirable thing, a rebellion of slaves to mock their masters. Back before it was gettin popular, Carnival shows was small enough to fit a backyard. It was an exhibition of culture, she say, a demonstration of freedom. Then, from the backyards, it poured into the streets. It gone nationwide, regionwide, worldwide. Now the descendants of the same slave masters would purchase airline tickets to join in the parades.

'It's an excuse to be reckless. It's obscenity,' Sister Mother use to say. 'Spitting in God's face.'

When I finally see it for myself, many years later, what I see mean nothin to me. A man laughin and dribblin the last of his pee on the sidewalk; a cotton candy man waddlin up and down the pavilion, steel handle constantly teeter-totterin in his grip; children runnin round with facepaint on; Sanskrit rubbin the front of his pants as he relished the endless rally of feathers and flab; men dressed as blue and red devils stick fightin come J'ouvert mornin. The streets would be fleeced with yellow and orange come Carnival Tuesday.

As the years went by, I watched Port-of-Spain grow. Buildings goin up, buildings breakin down, buildings waitin years to be torn down. The multiplex went up. The traffic jams got worse. The tunes from the music charts changed – different artistes, same shit. They painted pictures of dancers and steelpan players and endangered birds on the walls. Electronic billboards went up. Doubles vendors came and went. Snowcone men came and went. Coconut carts came and went. The rain fell harder. The dump piled higher. The skirts got shorter. Dignitaries rode past us in limousines. All it had between the suits and the tatters was a few sheets of board and metal.

Shit, the world was movin forward, but in this rusted village by the sea nothin ever change. Boys in their jockey-shorts still bathin in barrelwater. Sanskrit, despite the gamblin and alcohol, never managed to go totally broke. We'd have close calls and bad days, but the scrapyard was salvation. Even with food prices goin up year after year, I had a handsome amount saved up.

But the tables turned one day. Greaves went and get a heart attack and drop dead in his mistress' living room. Now, Sanskrit didn't give a shit bout Greaves, but he needed his pickup. Mrs. Greaves went and sell the damn thing and we couldn't get anybody else to help us. Monday wasn't Dump Day anymore, so Tuesday couldn't be Thanksgiving.

When I think back to this time, I think back to Father Anton's story. The Americans and the Russians. We had to innovate. But Sanskrit wasn't in no state of mind to do so. He bathe in puncheon and salt prunes for a month straight before we could even have a decent conversation. I was alone again. On the better days, he'd go down to the pubs and act the clown. Drunk men would throw him a dollar and he'd gyrate for them. Weird, seein a man become a wind-up monkey. He'd groove his neck like a chicken, a half-smoked cigarette hanging from his lips. It was funny. Everyone laughed. Even me.

But one day I dare to bring it up with him while he was countin his money, and he grab me and shove me against the wall. Scream right in my face, 'Let this be a lesson to you!' I didn't understand, but I was scared. Had no way I coulda predict his rage. It enter his body as fast as it used to leave. Like a spasm. One night, in his drunkenness, he ask me, 'I see you prayin. You believe in God?'

I take a long hard look at him before I respond. 'Yes.'

'It have a reason to think He believe in you, pardner?'

'I think we have to do what we have to do to keep good. Not much other choice.'

'Tell you, God make some of us sinners. But these sinners is different from the regular sinners, eh. These sinners He will forgive.'

'You sayin God make us commit sin?'

'Look at the world. Some of us hadda sin to survive. You ain't believe that?'

'But how God gon forgive you for a sin He make you commit?'

'Cause if God make you commit the sin, is not a sin, you hear?'

'That don't make sense.'

'You's one who believe God ain't insane. Listen, boy, God make the rules. He could be however He want to be. You believe He create everything, right?'

'Right.'

'But no man jack was round in the beginning. Didn't have no-one! But everyone believe in the story of how it happen! You ain't agree that is madness?'

'That is how it is.'

'Look, if that ain't madness, I ain't know what is.'

'It's not madness –'

'Just fuckin listen to what I say, nah!' he bawl as he hurl the burnin mosquito coil at me.

And I remember the exact words in my mind at the time: Did I fuckin miss something?

Sanskrit had always had his weird moments, but it was then I realized somethin was deeply wrong with him. Was like some star up there that was keepin him together, suddenly was misalign. Nothin to blame but the universe. At least, that's how I imagine he woulda put it.

I couldn't stay here at night. Spent most of it walkin along the shore, listenin to the bushes rustle as dogs scamper in and out of them. I looked at other people's houses. Sometimes I wished I took a souvenir from St. Asteria. I shoulda been a thief, even just for a day. Shoulda lift somethin from Mouse before she left, or somethin from the church. A hymnal. An altar cruet. A candle. All I had was memories and the naggin feelin that I make a terrible mistake. What had happened?

You had to realize somethin bout people once in a while – they're hardly ever what you hope them to be. Sanskrit was a broken man. Sometimes you needed the cracks to see the light inside of some people. Sometimes if you squinted, you coulda see the glow. But I was never sure for Sanskrit.

★

Me and Sanskrit started goin down to the avenue later on. Parkin was always hell on the avenue, so Sanskrit scoped out spots for patrons in exchange for a cool five-dollar fee. Sometimes he charge the white people twenty dollars. People paid him. They was comin out to spend money, anyway. This worked well for bout a week until Sanskrit started demanding money upon people's return. A ten-dollar charge for *security duty*.

He'd emerge from the street corner, groundin a cigarette stub under his heel. The ladies would huddle closer to their boy-friends, and the men would realize that this was a moment where the seconds counted. All laughter dissolved in the dark, all buzz sapped from the air. Everyone would suddenly get sober.

Sanskrit never *said* he would do anything to any of these people, yet they all paid. I ain't think what he was doin was a crime, but it was so easy that it damn well feel like one. Nobody wanted to have their night ruined. Nobody wanted to die, and when a man come up to you with that sly smile and them crazy eyes, you become suddenly aware that your body is just some mass of cells and tissue that could be shut off in a split second. And not one man jack wanted to die cryin like a baby. Not one man jack wanted their woman to be kill in front of them, even if they hated the bitch. Nobody wanted to die out in the street, where people could look out their windows and witness their body in spasms. No, everyone wanted the rest of their lives, one more night of drink and love. Nobody in their right mind woulda risk it.

One night, though, we come cross two fellas, and when Sanskrit come up to them for the money, they recognize him straight away. I recognize them too. They used to pay Sanskrit to dance and cluck like a chicken at a bar in St. James. They laughed and offered to double the bounty and pay him twenty to repeat the act for them. I felt like all my organs melted at that point. I knew some shit was gon go down.

Sanskrit lose it. He pick up a brick and smash the windscreen. Before the men could react, we burst off with a speed I didn't think we was capable of. Spits of rain come down as we cross the power plant. I didn't know where the hell we was runnin.

Worse yet, I didn't know if Sanskrit knew.

I remember that was the first time the thought crawl into my head – stayin with Sanskrit was goin to get me kill. But what was I gon do? I had nowhere else to go. For a while, I had it in my mind to save him. I could try.

But then, *she* show up.

'All in the name of love.'

★

Sanskrit come back to the house one night with a girl in his arm. Maybe a year or two older than me. Her hair was frizzy, electrified, and tie into a big rampant ball at the back. She looked like she just walk in from a storm. She had on an old black bubble dress, cut right above her thighs to reveal her ashy kneecaps. Her chest, broad and obscene, was stippled with baby powder. One strap was loose round her upper arm and breast, leaving the dress akilter and drooping. She was wearin a pair of red-tinted Ray-bans, even though it was near damn midnight. She had a spliff in her mouth, halfway smoked. She was standin one step outside the shack, framed by the door, engulfed in smoke.

'Boy, this is Shari,' Sanskrit tell me. 'She gon be livin here from now on.'

It happen just like that – I had no chance to say nothin. Just had to take it as it come. All hope of him goin back to anythin resemblin normal was way behind him now. I kept wonderin when it was gon be my turn to go. Seem like only a matter of time. The two of them use to fuck in the latrine after lunch, and late into the night. You could hear her callin him *Daddy* through the vents.

She was a savage. Used to kick the stray dogs that hang round the garbage heaps. Peed in full view of everyone. With her dress hiked up her waist and panties round her ankles, she squatted right there over the mud and dribbled urine into the tide. She'd walk round the house with her dress strap hanging loose, one nipple exposed as she lit up a post-sex cigarette. She was high outta her mind most of the time. More jumbie than human.

At nights, she hang round bars. Not the ones on the avenue, but the old pubs scattered along backroads of grime and vermin, where people get drunk the hardest. Where the men look like they beat their wives silly when they went home. She pickpocket a few of them while they piss in the drains. Broke into a few cars too, but she say it was hardly never worth it, that there was mostly little to find. She come straight out with all this. Wasn't no secret. She speak of it with pride.

She'd do this just to scrape together a few dollars to buy food from the vendors on the promenade – corn soup, aloo pies, shrimp roti, geera pork. When Sanskrit started goin with her, he never ask me to tag along, thank God.

Shari didn't actually live with us. She came and went as she please. But the damage was done. One day, she bring a gun for Sanskrit and call it a birthday present. From then on, the money was pourin in. He hit up every man jack walkin down every wrong road. It shock me at first when I learn what he was doin. This was the same man who toil for hours haulin copper from a dirt hill. Now, he coulda make twice the money in a matter of seconds. Why bother with honest dollars anymore? Never had to fire the gun. It become an addiction just like any other. Maybe he wasn't doin it for the money no more. He do it just to feel normal. When he score big, we use to go to this ramshackle Chinese restaurant. The lady coulda hardly talk a lick of English, but she was one of the nicest ladies I ever meet.

But then Sanskrit started talkin a bunch of shit bout how Chinese people don't use banks and how they hoard all their money in safes and under their beds. I was scared of him. I ain't never know what he was truly capable of. He ain't never kill nobody before, but murder wasn't off the table, I could tell you that. Was like what Rico say. It have shit you don't want to know you could do. I remember walkin into that empty restaurant one night, feelin certain that that Chinese lady wasn't goin to be breathin five minutes from then.

The air condition clicked and whirred. The tutti-fruity scent of air freshener fill my lungs. Sanskrit was fiddling with the back of his jeans, caressing the gun tuck against the edge of his spine. Dots of sweat along his neck. He bide the time, his eyes jumping back and forth along the assortments of three different kinda noodles and four flavours of pork. This lady was smilin at him whole time, just desperate for a sale.

This lady's life flashin through my mind. She was probably born in some dirty village halfway round the world where she and her husband get shack up near some pond teeming with mosquitoes. Maybe she'd see moments of sippin green tea on the weekend and biking to the grocery and gettin slapped round by old men. She'd see her husband smokin opium with strange shifty men. All the paperwork. The hours put in just to get here to this small island. All them moments would lead her to us. Just a ball on the roulette wheel.

'I come back, 'kay?' she say, still smilin. 'You call me when you ready order.'

I see Sanskrit reach for the gun. I feel like the whole world hold its breath at that moment. But before Sanskrit could make his move, a jingle sounded.

The door opened and a girl walked in. I tugged at his sleeve and say, 'C'mon man, we haveta get outta here. Ain't worth it.' It was a damn miracle – he agreed. We went home and all was well.

Another time, I end up following Sanskrit and Shari down a dead end. End of the line. Didn't even have no houses on that road, no inhabited ones, anyhow. This was a spot where all the pipers woulda come to get their fix-up, where only the stray cats could see them. I remember a mad vagrant in the distance preachin and cussin. A brown tailless cat come rubbin up against my ankle before disappearing behind an abandoned house. The same house that Shari was pointin Sanskrit to.

It was a house of legend – they use to call it the Douen Hole. Shari tell how it had a family that lived there, the Crichlows. Mr. Crichlow always had small plasters on his jaw from when he would cut himself shavin. He was a simple man, liked to sit outside with the radio and kaiso to keep him company. On the weekends, he'd bring home a small block of mora from the woodworks and spend his Sunday going at it with a little carving knife. He fashioned folklore creatures, mostly, or at least his own interpretations of them. The douens was his favourite. She say he carve them just as they was told to be – naked children with wide straw hats, feet facing backwards but Mrs. Crichlow find them hideous. She woulda nag her husband, asking why he busy himself carving ugly imps instead of forest animals and cherubs.

When Mrs. Crichlow wasn't sweepin the old cocoyea broom across the curls of whittled-off wood, Shari say she tend her garden of tomatoes and poinsettias. The daughter was always holed up in her room, headphones strapped on, forever in the zone. The son come and go whenever he please. Shari say how they had a bead curtain at the front door, and that they never let the lawn grow higher than their big toe. Simple people, was how she describe them.

When I first lay eyes upon the lawn, it was like it coulda wrap round my waist twice and swallow me up. The poinsettia garden musta been long dead. The windows was cracked, the house fallin apart – shit, it did already fall apart. From the distance, it ain't even look like a house, just a black, craggy mass.

Inside was like hell. The sound of men snoring in unison and gaggin while cockroaches and spiders scuttle in and out of their nostrils. You wouldn't think humans could let themselves get in such a position. Like baby pigs rootin in their own shit.

The Crichlow son was a naughty boy. He was involved in the coke trade. The parents knew bout their son but did nothing. They let him hide the stash in the dog kennel and latrine and operate from their dining room. Anyone ask them where the money was comin from, they just say, 'He doin a work for somebody.'

A bad deal went down one day and that somebody he was doin work for got mad. In that line of work, your severance package was a bullet in the eye. If you went the extra mile and really piss off the big man, then you coulda expect everyone important to you to lose *all* their benefits too.

Shari say the wooden douens lined up along a counter was the only things left from the house's former life. Everything else was destroyed, stolen or decomposed. Nobody bother to take the douens.

A girl did come walkin up to the door of the Douen Hole. She was wearin a red top, lookin like a rose that sprouted from the mouldy greys and browns round the house and yard. She didn't have to knock. The door open and a man emerge, shrouded in shadow. Never seen him. Never want to see him – but I know they call him just what he appear to be: Shadowman.

I ain't never wanted to have no business with Shadowman, or his money. He was the worst type of crook – the type that was once a police. The type who study the worst of both worlds. He wasn't the type to fuck round with. Ain't have nothin more unpredictable than a swarm of crackhead minions knowin you was the one who cut off the breast they was suckin from.

Shari kept her eye on Shadowman and the girl. Couldn't tell what she was buyin. Didn't care. All that matter was that she had money. A girl dressed like that in a place like this – all I coulda say is that she had problems. Never known why rich youth would put themselves in positions like that, but I see it all the time.

At the end of the road, past the cul-de-sac, was a walkway up to a hill. 'She does go up there to smoke,' Shari say.

'How you know that?' Sanskrit ask.

'Because I does go there too.'

'So, what's the plan?'

'I say, we pay the bitch a visit.' Shari grinned.

I take a step back in protest but I didn't say nothin. I didn't know why I was out there with them – we just end up there somehow. They didn't tell me no plan to mug no rich girl. I wasn't in no mood to be kindlin my own death. I turn and take the long walk back to the shack.

A few hours later, Sanskrit bust through the door, bloodied up, the little self-respect he had beat outta him. The kinda beatin he receive wasn't cause he stick his dick in crazy. Somehow, crazy went and stick its dick in him. He never talk bout it. The man ain't sleep the whole day after that. I stay up with him the whole time. I was worried. If something was to happen to him, well, crapaud smoke my pipe.

He pace round his bed, his steps uncertain – like he thought the ground would crack and collapse beneath him. Then he'd fly into fits of rage, violently beating the pins-and-needles outta his legs and smashing the necks of beer bottles before shattering them against the wall.

But one day he wake up calm. Wistful, he sit me down and tell me that things woulda be all right. That we still had money – despite the things he had to do to get it. For a while, he was sleepin sound, eatin proper. So, I was thinkin, yeah, what don't kill does fatten. Shari wasn't round during them times. Whenever I ask bout her, he just say, 'Pardner, she's a kinda gal. Like to play mas, but fraid powder.'

One night, he lean over and say, his voice halfway sleepy and halfway drunk, 'Most everybody I ever know end up dead. What you think bout that?'

'I don't understand.'

'I might be a hazard to your health. Ever wonder that?'

One day, at dusk, he coax me back down that dead end road. The one where Shadowman's house was. Anything so he wouldn't fly into a rage again. I didn't know he had the gun on him till the breeze swoop down and I see it outlined against his jersey. He stand there eyeing the house. A fishy reek was trickling out from it. As the wind blew again, I swear the whole house shift – like it was alive. The house eaves flap and knock against rusty galvanize.

The streetlight flicker over his face. This was a man with a appetite for death – kamikaze, jihad, whatever the fuck you want to call it. I just didn't want to be caught in the crossfire. I kept my eye on him. Really couldn't tell if he was a part of this world anymore, or if he cared. I grab his arm and whisper to him, 'You ain't in your senses. Come, I gonna go back to the promenade.'

'Let me go, boy,' he say, pullin his arm away. 'I ain't stupid.'

He plod across the overgrown weeds and bracken and knock on the door.

As it open, the shadow engulf him. I wasn't sure if Sanskrit step inside by himself, or if the shadow pull him inside. I hid my ass behind an old rusted sedan. My heart was beatin fast-fast-fast. I swear everything else slowed down during that moment. The eaves tilting. The shadows slanting. The air laden with hot moisture. A stray dog was hacking behind me.

I was sweating, waitin, for the gunshot. For whatever signal there was gon be to start fuckin runnin.

But there was none. Sanskrit come back into view, clean and intact. The door shut behind him. I thought he was gon come back to me, but instead he hurry up to the hill. I went after him all the way up the dusty path. I know at the top was two benches, side by side, that overlook the boatyard.

There was someone else there – Shari. There was moonlight

but it was trap behind a cloud. I couldn't see her face, but I knew the hair. Sanskrit took a seat next to her.

'So you livin then,' she say to him. She was slurring, high. She wrung her long, dainty arms.

'Alive and kickin.'

'What you doin up here?' Then she notice me. 'Your lil friend decide to come up too. Cute.'

'The breeze nice. A man can't enjoy some breeze?'

'Used to come out here when my mother act up at home, you know.' Her voice lowered. I wasn't sure if she was sad or mellow. She keep staring out over the sea, as if some jumbie was gon jump out from the brine.

'So, you bring anything?' she ask.

'We ain't gon talk bout last time?'

'Things like that does happen. People feel they own me, but nobody own me. People get jealous, boy.' She lean closer. 'You know how it is. All in the name of love.'

'Love, eh?' Sanskrit say. 'I ain't have nothin to say to that.'

'If you have somethin to say, just say it.'

He shake his head. 'Not really necessary.'

'I ain't mean talk to me,' she say. 'Talk to yourself, man. Let it out.'

'I ain't in the habit of talkin to myself. You should take your own advice, gal. You sound like you's the one who have problems.'

'Problems? We all have problems, boy. But I managin good with mine, don't worry yourself.'

'You sure? Because, Shari, you soundin like the island sinkin.'

'You find so?'

'Yeah. Is not somethin a man could hear and keep quiet bout.'

She bow her head. 'I know you just playin. Look, I know you mad bout the other night. We could talk bout it. Is not my fault. I ain't with the man or nothin. You know, me and you, we strong. You ain't know that?'

'Too well.'

She paused. 'Is just that the man feel he does run things.'

'I was a gamblin man, you know. When I still had my folks, I use to steal money from them just to go out and lose it. Had a speech my pa give me before he kick me out. He say the world like one of them roulette tables. A gamblin man just doomed to place bets and watch the little ball click and clack against the red and black and wait to see the outcome.'

'We ain't have no control over any of it?'

'The ball? No, no, no. But you could control how much you willin to put down.'

'So, how much you willin to throw down now?'

'Nothing.'

'What you mean?'

'My pa tell me not to be a gamblin man no more. He tell me to be the croupier.'

'I woulda figure the croupier to be God.'

'Nah, God just own the casino. God in the backroom just chillin, swivellin in the office chair. He know all the chips go back to Him eventually. No matter how you want to cut it, gal, the house always wins.'

'The house always wins. Huh.' She click her tongue. A gruff barking echoed faintly from somewhere down the track. Sanskrit batted the back of his neck. His sudden movement made Shari jump, but she quickly regained her composure, lookin back down at the black sea. She ask him, 'How you think someone could get to that level? To be the croupier, I mean.'

'I think they become one at the exact moment they figure out how to be one. You have to be able to turn that wheel no matter how much the people bet. No hesitatin if a person put their life, their children, their soul on the line. No hesitatin, even knowin that person could destroy another human life just by you turnin that wheel. But three things remain certain. The wheel must spin. The ball is random…'

'…and the house always wins,' she finish the sentence.

His mouth broke into a wide grin. 'But I slip up. I went back to bein a gamblin man. I take a gamble with you.'

'You win or you lose?'

'What you think?'

She sucked her teeth as she leaned forward, elbows on knees – hangin her head as if she was goin to vomit. 'I think you talk too much shit. I know you vex. Just give it a while and things gon go back to normal. Me and you strong.'

He shrug. 'Well, if you say so, you say so.'

She got up from the bench, kickin the ground, dirt crunchin beneath her soles. She was still nothin but a silhouette. 'If you ain't have nothin good for me,' she tell him, 'then I ain't really want to talk to you right now. Hope you ain't mind.'

She unclenched her fists and hunch over. He got up from the bench and put his palm on her back. I got up too. I thought that was it. That we was gonna go and this night would be over.

'I holdin,' he tell her, 'but we can't do nothin here.'

She snap to attention. 'Where then?'

A screakin sound come on the breeze. I turn my head and realise it was a swing just up the road. The plastic seat swung back and forth, as if some phantom child was sittin and moping on it. It went screak-screak with each graze against the corroded steel.

'Come,' Sanskrit say, and he took her hand and led her to the swing. He motion for me to follow.

The moon come out from behind a cloud and I see she settle in the swing and hold the ropes tight. He kneel before her and put his hand in his pocket and take out a pinch of coke. He hold it up to her nose and with one sniff, it was gone. He then went behind her and give her a light push. Just a tap. 'You different, boy,' she was tellin him. I sensed the affection in her tone. He pushed her again. She say with uncommon sweetness, 'Which other man would stick with he woman like this?'

'Well, gal, today for me, tomorrow for you.'

He push her again.

'I ain't know what you mean.'

'I here for you. I expect you to be here for me.'

'We should get married, boy. Right here.'

'Weddings should take place in some place that's pure. It dirty out here. The grass ain't trim. Weeds all over. People leavin their boxes of half-eaten fry chicken. Dog shit pile up all over the place. This place too filthy for a weddin.'

'Fittin for my life then, eh? Walkin down an aisle of fry chicken and dog shit,' she say, laughing.

Laughing too, he pushed her again.

'This is it right here, boy,' she say. 'The damn life self.'

Two stray dogs scamper past, chasin some ghost.

'Tell me more bout this dog-shit weddin you want to have, gal.'

She laugh. He push her twice while she was still thinkin. 'It goin to have to be rainin.'

He push.

She continued, 'All the guests gon get wet.'

He push.

'Then they gon all leave, you know?'

He push harder. She grip the ropes tight as she arced up and down.

'And you can't show up, boy!'

Screak.

'Cause we hadda have a runaway groom!'

Screak-screak.

'What you think?' She raise her voice. 'You like that?'

'I do.' His hand shoot into his pocket and he pull out somethin small and shiny.

She was comin down. She was arcin down.

She arced down right against him.

'Jordon, hold she, boy!' he shout.

I ain't even think bout what I was doin. I wrapped my arms round her and press my forehead against her back so hard that it musta felt like a headbutt. He clasp the object in his hand tight, and under the moonlight, I see what it was. A syringe. He stick the needle in her neck and press down on it. Whatever cocktail it had in it now surging through her bloodstream. She flail like a chicken as she fall to the ground, gasping for breath.

The light finally fall on her face, on her head as it jerk, on her teeth as they scrape against the dirt.

Sanskrit kneel beside her and tip her chin towards him. Then he forced his lips against hers, the needle still wiggling, still wedged in the blood vessel, still pokin outta her neck.

I bawl out, 'Sanskrit, what the fuck! *What the fuck you do!*'

Easy way to kill somebody who already killin theyself.

The dogs scamper past us, still chasin the ghost. I watched them disappear in the distance as he spit on her dead body, kicking dirt in her hair.

'Run, especially if it have nothin to run to!'

★

Was an Ash Wednesday night. At least, I think so. I can't remember the order of things or what was nightmare, what was real. The plan was for me to hit up this high-end bar on the avenue. I'd chat up some of the tourists and Sanskrit would spring their wallets.

Never know what Sanskrit was liable to do after I see what he do to Shari. What was I gon do? Everyday I pass boys, my age, kick outta their homes. House dogs suddenly waking up to find themselves strays, out there in the street with no kinda stomach to eat off the pavement.

Sanskrit know I was scared, and he know I needed him. He take full advantage of that. He also know that no matter if you was a young, hot-blooded jammette or an old, rich man with a pocket full of Viagra, everybody who was out on Carnival wanted to let loose the demons within them. Every man jack had the permission to sin, and nobody could say shit to them.

I remember raising my head from the counter after one too many – not on my tab, thankfully. My head hurt, like it was gon collapse in on itself. I didn't feel well at all. Feel like I was gon faint. Feel like I was everywhere at once, like I was tricklin outta myself, cross the bar, stainin the carpet, under the door, right into the street. Feel like my soul was bouncin round the walls, curvin up to the ceiling. Just remember everything bein blurry, wibbly-wobbly. Just shapes. Soft outta-focus shapes – all mixed up – some things sped up – and some things in slow motion – even my thoughts. Thought bout people wakin up and prayin to god and kneelin before five dollar calendars or settin the milk on their lingams – scrubbin up leftovers of powder on Ash Wednesday and feelin so grateful for the day. Wished I could wake up and know what its like to be grateful to wake up.

A hand reached out to touch my shoulder. Looked at the man attached to the hand. He was smilin at me – white man lookin bout fifty, head not completely grey, little crows feet formin by the eyes – wearin a cheap suit and clip-on tie but still managin to look sharp in it. His breath was a meld of alcohol and vanilla – uppity American accent.

'So farmboy, my niece likes to watch this cartoon, *Winnie the Pooh*. You know the thing right?'

'Know what thing?'

'There's a character in there who's always rundown and miserable. It also happens that he's a depressed ass…'

So I'm here thinking… depressed *because* he was an ass? Did that have anything to do with it? He had friends who liked him… Didn't seem to have any real troubles. So where did it stem from?

He laugh and say, 'Damn it, I have so much to be thankful for.'

'I'm sorry,' I say, 'I dunno what you talkin bout.'

'You know him, farmboy… the donkey…'

He looked at my glass.

'That was a special, special drink, manna from heaven, apple from Eden…'

I look at him.

'Who the fuck are you again?'

He laughs and ask, 'Feelin it yet?'

What the fuck! Who the hell is this person?

I saw myself from the outside for a second – just there slumpin over a bar with a row of men chatterin with each other and tracin fingers along each others sleeves – all *bullermen!* – and then me, lookin like a dirty runaway fuckboy with sweat stains on my armpits and no money in my pocket – ripe for the pickin.

'What's your name again?'

'Let's not go there, farmboy. It's much more thrillin if we just remain strangers… Don't deliberate… You'll enjoy life more… Just have fun, have a gay old time.'

I cocked my head at him.

'Have a gay old time, you know, like the Flintstones.'

'The fuck?'

'You don't have a TV, farmboy? Flintstones… Gay old time… Fuck it, nevermind.'

He light up a cigarette, take a drag and then give it to me.

Take a pull, lungs get hot.

'Look at all these fags in here, farmboy...' Makes me sick. Everyone in here is in heat. Places like this could give you cancer... Fags just like to flock together and bask in heat... Call it the greenhouse effect or whatever.'

He stared at a couple at the other end of the bar – young fella with an old man – playin with each others fingers, smilin like ladies in a spa commercial.

'Look at him, farmboy. Probably married, probably going to shit out his liver later – forget about the pancreas... That's already gone to hell... Sky high cholesterol. Probably has children too. Wife's a blimp! and he's going to go home later tonight and fuck the hell out of her *ha ha ha!*'

He raised his glass to the man.

'Cheers!' He continue. 'I never bothered to get married... Never even bothered to get a girlfriend... not like the rest of these old queers, because I know there was going to come a point when it was either fuck or walk... All these sad old men in here... They're all in decline, you know. They know they wasted it all on pussy they're pretending wasn't pussy... They know it's too late... And lemme tell you the way of the world, farmboy... There's nothing worse than too late...'

'Have to go piss...'

Got up, stumble across the room, the room still wobbly shapes, blurry colours and muddled features. Enter the men's room, drag up to the sink, gag, spit, vomit a bucket of gunk – and then some more.

Felt better after. I looked at the vomit forming in the shape of a brown butterfly in the white ceramic. Watched as the butterfly decomposed and slid down the drain. Faceless men adjusted their crotches at the urinals. Bodies fat and thin and crooked all lined up, juicing out neverending streams of piss.

Went back to the bar and sat next to the American. He still had the cigarette drooping from the corner of his mouth, running a safety clip under his fingernails. Still tastin the vomit in my throat.

'Hey farmboy, want to be my son?' he whisper to me. 'You

could let me adopt you.' He took a drag on the cigarette and ask me, 'What kind of child do you think I'd want?'

I kept lookin out for Sanskrit, but that fucker was nowhere to be seen. The American raise his eyebrows at me. Playing along, I tell him, 'Obedient.'

'You wanna go somewhere quiet?'

All I wanted to do was go. Leave. Get outta that shit-hole. I wasn't thinkin straight. So I nod, and tell him, 'Yes.'

'Yes, *who?*'

'What?'

'*Daddy.*' The word hiss outta his mouth like steam.

I swallowed hard. 'Yes, Daddy.'

Next thing I know, I find myself in some fancy hotel. Can't remember how that happen. I didn't know where the fuck I was. I wasn't suppose to be here. Never was suppose to leave the bar. Where the fuck was Sanskrit? Somethin was wrong. Somethin was wrong with me. I was gettin all mixed up. Now, I was in this bright golden room.

This is it, I remember thinkin. This must be hell.

I remember hearin running water and faint music. He was takin a shower. The radio was on. I got up to change the station, but I coulda barely walk without wobbling. I fell to my knees.

I looked up. The door slammed and the American busted out naked. His hair was drippin wet. 'Clothes still on?' he say.

'Look, take it easy.'

'No reason to be nervous.'

'But –'

'Every boy does it. Take off your pants. Let Daddy help you.'

'I can't stay here.'

He pushed me back on the bed and held me down. Soap suds runnin down the sides of his body. He licked his lips. Skin brushin against mine, feelin like scales. Reptilian – flaky grey skin. He got busy unbuttonin my shirt, licking the sparse curls of my chest hair before flippin me over.

As he did, his voice morph. Went high like a woman's voice, muffled, as if it had to slide through coalsmoke. I turned round and saw her. Kitty. Sister Katherine Ines Lewis. Back from the dead. She smile at me. I watched the pink warmth from her complexion flare and then drain away. She was on top of me, me lyin belly-down, her full breasts pursed against her habit, pressed over the edge of the bed. She looked more witch than nun.

I was ten years old again, dengue-stricken, frog-voiced, skin ballooning with heat. I had it bad – thought I was gon die. You feel the pain suckin at your bones. It's so bad that you feel everything fall away from you. Parts that you take for granted – bones, joints, cartilage, tissue fluid – they're all rebellin against you. Couldn't move.

'We have to take your temperature,' she say, in sing-songy anticipation. We? You and who else? She produce a rectal thermometer. Small and sterile-white. The one for babies. Designed for an age that didn't know embarrassment. She smoothed my hair back, pulled the blanket off me and wiped me with a towel. Couldn't move, felt as if chained to a steel pole. She leaned over, pushing her knee against my ankle.

The voice went deep down. Weight pressin down on me. The American held me down harder. I was floppin round like a fish outta water. The words coulda barely come out. 'Get offa me. Get offa me.' Just broken whimpers. I turn my neck to watch him. The ceiling fan rotate round the golden light, like corbeaux circling the midday sun. The man was a giant snail crawling over my back. He lick me like a thirsty dog.

He plant a slow curve of kisses from one shoulder blade to the next. I tried to break free, but he wouldn't let go of my wrist.

Again, I tell him, 'I ain't playin.'

He snorted like a horse. I could feel his prick rubbin against the back of my thigh.

'Rectal temperatures are the most accurate,' Kitty say as she took my pants off. But I was a big boy, too old for this. Too old to have this thing shoved up my ass.

She put me on my back and hoisted my legs up.

All the blood rush to my head. Was like a gush of nails fell into my eyes. Coulda see nothin but shapes now, formless colours dangling in red space. The shame suckin my bones now more than the dengue.

'You're burning up,' she told me. I was too confused to do anything, to say anything, to even grunt. I just remember the feelin of falling. My head cocked to the side and drool leaked down my jaw.

I arched my neck. 'Get offa me. Get offa me.' The words still struggled to get past his snortin horse-lust. Looked at the window again. Couldn't believe it at first but I saw it. I squinted. It was *there*. It was *me*, staring back. Silently. Unblinking. A mannequin version of me watchin with dead eyes at this naked white-legged, white-bodied rottin creature latching onto me.

'Be a man! Be a man!' he was yellin, rubbing his palm against my balls.

I lashed his hand away and spring on him. He went runnin to get his belt on the floor. Then he started whippin the room like a madman. Whippin the carpet, whippin the mirror, whippin the bed!

'Daddy's going to beat you, boy! Daddy's going to fix you, fix you up good – fix you *proper!*'

He hit me a good three or four times on my back before he toss the belt away and pin me down again. Squirming, I turned back to the window. The mannequin was gone.

I stopped flailing, stopped resisting. I let him splay me out on my back. Arms out. He rip my pants off. Pull my legs apart. I couldn't move, couldn't move, couldn't move! He hoisted my legs up like a baby ready to get powdered, and started kissin and lickin and suckin my asshole. He went *mmm-mmm-mmm*, his tongue lapping at it like a thirsty dog – desperate to get an erection outta me. He was lickin, lickin, lickin. *Mmm-mmm-mmm*.

It hurt. It hurt when she put the thermometer in. I clenched my asshole tight against it – probably the only muscle I coulda move at this point. Sent shivers down my legs. The spurt of blood burble up my groin and shot my prick right up. The rest of my body was in rigor mortis. I can't remember much else. I don't want to.

But I had to stay here. Had to fight it through.

Couldn't pretend to be somewhere else.

Couldn't close my eyes. Moments like this, the seconds matter. Moments like this, you have to save yourself.

Take the chance to know and remember the smell of darkness, then save yourself.

I wish I fight the bitch. I wish I kick her. *Fuck!*

I wish I done something. Anything!

Why didn't I scream? Why didn't I tell nobody? I'm sure she didn't stick nothin up Rey's asshole. Or Rico's asshole. Or Quenton's asshole!

'My daddy dead,' I told the American, his tongue still trailing the perimeter of my ass. I pull my foot back and start kickin him right in his nose. He gag. Ack! *Ack!* I drag him off the bed, across the room. I reach for the belt, reach and reach until I get it. Got up fast while he was still on the ground. Held both ends of the belt tight. Wrapped it round his neck and started *pullin, pullin, pullin*. We fall backwards on the bed, two naked bodies slippery with sweat.

I pulled the belt harder – he still breathin – he still kickin – his neck already snap but somehow he was still there kickin! Was already too late for him.

Another whole minute of struggle and the fucker was still alive, still clawin at the belt locked round his neck. I look round the room. The window gazing into nothing, bursting out of nothing. The room was expanding. I hearin bone after bone breakin but somehow *this fucker is still alive*.

I finally let go.

He fall to the floor and started to shudder. Then he get back up – head tiltin to the side, like a snapped twig – wheezin, speakin words not of any human tongue, the light fading fast from his eyes but his body's there, still moving, still fightin the inevitable.

The lights fadin fast. Darkness now.

This must be hell.

The groanin *ungh ungh ungh*. Started feelin my way round, hit my knee against his shin, his hand shoot to grab my balls – he start twistin them so hard that the pain jet right to my eyes. Bite my tongue until it bleed.

Ungh ungh ungh.

Fuck, he comin this way – he comin this way – the man who think he is my daddy comin this way – he comin to beat me.

I feel round more. Pushed a door open – runnin water – shower still runnin – groanin gettin louder and faster.

Ungh-ungh-ungh.

Feelin round the bathroom – passed my hand over the toilet – hugged it

I shoved my face in the toilet – a hand grabbin my foot – it's pullin me. Pullin my head out of the toilet. Something's tryin to drag me out. I'm kickin and kickin and kickin. Then kick and snap somethin – a loud squeal – the hand let go of my foot. Rush back to the toilet, plunge my head back in the bowl.

Swim and swim until I see the light – swimmin towards the light – brilliant white light – reach the surface and take a deep breath. Open my eyes – darkness.

Silence again.

Safety.

Sightless.

Soundless.

Swimmin in a black ocean over black coral – sinkin – sinkin with no arms to make it back to the surface.

Tryin to speak but couldn't hear myself.

Maybe a secret opening somewhere – a trap door out of this place. Hear a dog barkin this whole time – stomach churning – swellin – gettin heavy like a bullfrog's belly – the pain radiating from my stomach to asshole.

'Sant – wake up fool – wake the hell up!'

Recognized the voice – opened my eyes – found myself some bushes.

The voice cut through the haze again: 'You walkin in your sleep, fool! You talkin in your sleep, fool!'

Elroy?

A figure moved in the shadows. A man.

'Sant, Sant, what you doin?'

'Elroy, that you?' I cuffed the back of his head and my fist went right through him.

Grab his collar tight.

'Elroy? Tell me what happenin!'

'God comin for you, fool, God comin for your ass!'

Cuffed at his neck again.

'God comin! God comin! God don't sleep!'

Then I stopped.

I counted.

One.

Two.

Three.

I realize it wasn't no Elroy. Blood leakin down my chin. Each time I swallow, I swallowed blood. Passed my tongue along my gums, put my fingers in my mouth and pull out a tooth only hangin from two threads of gum. Spittin flesh from under my tongue, chunks of flesh ripped out by my own teeth.

The ground shook again.

Looked back and nothin is there. Just black. Trudged further into the bush. Licked the blood off my bottom lip. Kissed the wounds on my arms. The more I walked, the narrower the path get. Black trees crowd round me, threatenin to block my way. When I came to the clearin, I saw her.

Mouse.

As big as God.

Sound asleep. Unclothed. Her body stretchin all across the land. Her face lookin like sunrise expanding over a mountain range. Her skin's pores as wide as mole burrows. Her hair loose like massive black drapes hanging from the clouds.

I climbed up by her hair and stood on her forehead. Slid down each eyebrow. Did a dance on her cheeks. Lay on her lips and looked at the stars. Climbed down her neck. Ran circles round the right nipple. Then the left nipple. Then I crawl to the navel and squeezed down into it.

It was dark inside. I grope round to find my way. Had a small passageway. So I got on all fours and started to creep. The passage got narrower and narrower the further I went. No turnin back now. Moistness on my palms. Tiny green lights glittered round me, hovering like candleflies. There was music playin. Soft music, curling into a fuzzy whorl into my ear.

Then I felt something like smooth muscle fittin neatly round me. I realize I wasn't even crawlin no more. It was pushin me along. But not too fast. Lay on my chest and let it propel me headforth. Like a horizontal pool-diver, my entire body coated with stickiness. A bright white light in the distance blinded me.

I closed my eyes. My heart beat faster with each second I got closer. I moved through the light. I saw it through my eyelids.

'Let God have somethin to thank me for.'

★

I woke up with the harsh bright fluorescent light right above me. I was in some kinda public health centre. I couldn't open one of my eyes – musta swell shut. My clothes was a mess – pants caked with mud, bloodstains on my collar, clippings of grass on my sleeves. A salty bloody tang in my mouth, hackin up foamy globs of phlegm. Each breath cut its way up my windpipe as if it brought up metal dust from my lungs. My flesh frail, my bones and joints crackin, I feel I reach some absolute in human misery.

The doctor, keeping his head down the whole time as he talk, ask me how much I'd been drinkin. I had to let his words swim round my head for a while before I could make them out. I shake my head. I wasn't sure how long I'd been out of it – still don't know. Was it just the one night? Who had brought me in? I was sweatin like crazy. A nurse came up and ask me if I use drugs. I tell her no, which was the truth. Then struggle to add, 'Not to my knowledge.'

I didn't want to stick around. I didn't want no police askin me questions. I hated clinic beds. Felt like I was lain down on a damn ironing board. The cold steel shocked my skin. I didn't want to stay, but I didn't want to bolt outta there either. It woulda look suspicious, and I wasn't sure I was back to normal. Everything seemed all mixed up. Didn't know what could still happen. Last place I needed to end up was the madhouse.

I get up to go to the toilet. The nurse offer to escort me, but I lash away her arm. Was a reflex, but I didn't want nobody touchin me – fuck that. Was still feelin dizzy like hell. The floor seemed too low, like my feet had to stretch down to reach it. Doors was too far. The little toilet room feel like a damn hallway. I couldn't even sit properly without fallin over. The fluorescent tube blinkin like a strobe. Made my head hurt. I look at myself in the mirror. They put a bandage over my nose. One of my eyes was a puckering circle of blood-purple, like some wormridden fruit. I let the tap run and splashed water over my face. Wet the edge of my fist and tried to scrub the dirt out of my pants. How I end up there?

Sanskrit set me up. He pimp me out. The American drug me. I was right. I shoulda listen to myself. Stayin with Sanskrit was gon kill me.

I was afraid I'd die here, in the toilet. Must've been some kinda giddiness set in, but I honestly thought I was done for. I even wonder if I was dreamin, if this was one of them moments before death. It feel like that, it really did. Totterin off the edge of existence, barely hangin on. Just enough to see your life under the flickering light of a toilet. I was plummeting. One less stray dog to worry bout.

Then I hear the sound of madness outside. Shouts, cries, howls. Heard a woman and a man pleadin, 'They fuckin shoot him! They fuckin shoot him!' and the doctor responding, again and again, in the same rehearsed monotone, 'We can't do anything for him here.'

The nurse was tellin them, 'Listen, you have to wait for the ambulance. We can't do anything for him here.'

I opened the toilet door to see the commotion. Two nurses was tryin to calm the frantic pair while a third was tryin desperately to strap the wounded man to a stretcher. Wasn't to roll the man nowhere, I was guessin, just to restrain him and bide time till the buck pass to the paramedics. The woman was young, dark, skin showin, lookin like she just writhe out of a fete. She was on her knees, holding the wounded man's wrist, blubberin out Hail Marys. The man was wearin a red string vest, his hair tied in a bushy bun. Both of them had blood on their hands. The wounded man had shit himself at some point. I coulda see the curds of brown drippin down his legs. Seen it before the stench of faeces start leakin into the adjacent rooms. Jesus Christ, what a horrible place to die.

'Give him somethin, nah!' the woman shout at the nurses.

The doctor was busy rubbing peppermint concentrate under his nose. The shit smell was unbearable.

'We could only stop the bleeding for now –' one of the nurses say, as the wounded man started to convulse on the stretcher. One of the nurses, a young one, probably not a half year into the job, began to cry. She was cryin and dry-heavin at the same time. The woman let the man's wrist fall out of her grip and all of them launch back, like the man was bout to blow the fuck up.

'Father Lord in heaven!' the other nurse, much older, cry out.

I ain't gon lie. I expected him to explode too. Blow a geyser of blood and pus right up to the ceiling. As the chaos swelled, I could only think one thing. This was my shot. One of the nurses left her wallet at the desk. I swipe it on my way out and never look back.

I made the long way back cross Port-of-Spain to Sanskrit place. It take a while, I tell you, but I make it back in one piece. Walkin back is probably what is clearest in my mind. I ain't have no idea what the time was, but the roads was empty and clean. I remember the sidewalks almost look like they was sparklin. The concrete was cold and dry and it ain't have no sound blowin cross the street except my own footsteps.

I didn't know what to expect when I got back, but I had nowhere else to go. Fuck, time was skippin ahead. The whole damn sky was fallin on top of me. I remember just standin in the street, lookin up at the lighthouse and thinking it was looking down upon me, judging me. It was trying to set me straight. Whatever delusion that was still floatin round, it was gone. Honestly, I was hopin the whole thing was a misunderstandin. I was willin to believe that lie. I was willin to believe it for now – at least until I could get the fuck out of this place. I didn't know where I was gon go, but I couldn't stay here, not if I wanted to live.

Still, I couldn't just go. I don't know why it was so hard to walk away from something that was killing me. I walk away from St. Asteria, why not this? Shit, I coulda just run, but I had blood on me. Rapist blood, but still – white man rapist blood. I had to make sure me and Sanskrit was square.

As I walk in the shack, he latch onto my collar. 'The fuck you doin here?' he spit out at me.

Before I coulda say anything, he slap me.

I hesitated. I don't know if it was still the drugs. I wanted to explode but I couldn't. Instead of demandin explanations, I suddenly felt an urge to apologize. But before I could say anything, he lift me off my feet. 'You's a fuckin psychopath! Jah!' He shove me against the wall and I fell against a chair.

I kick at him. 'You leave me by myself.'

'I ain't leave you nowhere! Who tell your ass to follow that man? That was never part of the plan!'

'You drug me up!'

'I ain't drug up shit, pardner! You fuckin kill the man! And you come and drag your hot tail back here for the police to find you, eh!' He pull the cutlass out from under the mattress and smack my face with the broad side. 'Get your ass outta here!'

'You leave me there to die!'

I block a second blow with my arm. My stomach soured as he raise the cutlass a third time.

Just as he was bout to bring it down on me again, I scamper to the other side of the room. He rush to me and slam me against the wall. He yank open a drawer and pull out his gun. He hiss, 'Me and you done!'

Still on the ground, I slide my foot at his ankle and he come topplin down. The gun hit the floor. I scramble to get it. Back on my feet. I point the gun at him. He look up at me, right up at the barrel. My hand was tremblin. The metal was heavy and cold in my hand.

Then there was a heavy knockin on the door, so hard that it rattle the walls.

The gun fall from my hand.

The rattlin sounded again. I try to move but my body was paralysed.

We fix our eyes on the door. No knockin this time. Just mumblin.

Then a loud crack.

Sanskrit fell to the ground howling, blood spurtin from his kneecap. A bullet had smash right into the joint. The door bust open and three men stood, silhouetted against the moonlight. Du-rags, corn rows, tattoos. And glocks cocked back, of course. The works. 'Get on the fuckin floor!' one of them yell out.

As I press my chest against the ground, I look up. I nearly shit my pants as I saw the camo NY cap. The name just come out. 'Quenton?'

He step forward and I coulda see him clear now. He raise the bill of the cap. It *was* Quenton.

'Shit,' he say, lettin out a nervous laugh. 'That you, boy? Sant, that you? What you doin here with this nigger?'

Sanskrit shoot a confused look at me.

'What *you* doin here?' was all I could ask.

'This nigger here ain't pay his taxes. So the taxman come –' He stop mid-sentence and approach me, lookin at the blood on my collar. 'What the fuck happen to you?' He then notice the gun on the floor. He squinted at Sanskrit. 'What the fuck happenin here?'

'Quenton.' All I could say was his name.

Quenton pointed the gun at Sanskrit. 'This man do this to you, Sant? This man bloody you up so?'

Sanskrit and I exchange glances. From then I knew the power I held.

Sanskrit shoot a look at me, probably thinkin I set him up.

Quenton say, 'We just here to collect the tax.' He flip the mattress over and take the money I was keepin in a small crocus bag.

'That is my savings, Quenton.'

'Yeah?' he say. 'I suppose to give it back?'

I didn't say nothin.

He then say, 'This motherfucker scam we, hoss. Can't let shit like that slide.'

I say, 'Is not his money, though.'

Sanskrit started blubberin. Quenton smacked him in his head with the pistol. He say, 'Hear what, Sant. You want your money? Take it. But we bustin him right here point-black in the head if that is how you playin it.' He toss the crocus bag on the floor.

'It have to come to this?'

'The man have to pay.'

This was it. I felt a jolt of sympathy. The man did take me in. He take care of me. He feed me, he show me the ropes. He let me crawl on his back and we cross the river together. But there were his sins, his numerous transgressions. He use me as a pawn. He involve me in shit, but I never thought he woulda make the move to sacrifice me. So, shit, who was the scorpion and who was the frog here?

Quenton say, the gun still on Sanskrit, 'Fuck, boy, I probably clairvoyant. I wasn't comin in here with no mind to kill nobody. But look like I might change my mind.'

I had the opportunity. I had to take it. Easy way to kill somebody who already killin theyself. God send Quenton for him. God send Quenton to save me. It ain't up to nobody here to question the strangeness of God's mercy.

'The man was movin to kill me,' I say.

'That is true?' Quenton ask Sanskrit.

'N… No,' Sanskrit stutter.

'So he is a liar then?'

'No.'

'Good.'

Quenton smiled. He click his tongue and pull the trigger. The ragged spark filled the room for a second, and that was that. Sanskrit didn't die right away. But I saw him die. We all stood in that room and waited for him to die, his gnarled and knobbly fingers twitchin for a full minute. When he was still, I become jumpy. Giddy. He was dead, but I had the feelin he woulda just spring back up, just like the American. Coulda be the drugs still coursin through my blood, but I couldn't stop thinkin back to the fucker in the hotel. How he just wouldn't die! Break his neck sideways and he was still alive!

Couldn't risk that shit happenin again, so I say to Quenton, 'Shoot him again.'

There was something about observing death. It felt like light burstin out of me. Quenton say to me, 'You gone mad, Sant?'

'He ain't dead,' I say, even though I knew he was.

One of Quenton's partners say, 'The man done meet he maker, boy.'

Quenton then say to the man, 'You feelin for a doubles, boy? Have anywhere close to here that does be open this hour?'

Before he left, he ask, 'Sant, why you had skip out just so, boy?'

'To get a head start on life.'

Quenton laughed. 'Well, you just get a next one. Get the fuck out from this place and do somethin good. I ain't savin nobody for free, bitch. You owe me, eh. Let God have somethin to thank me for.' Then he was out the door.

I watch as Quenton scoop up a handful of rubble from the ground and fling it into the water. I saw his back in the moonlight. He had two large keloids near his shoulder blades. Knife wounds? Cutlass chops? Scars from where they cut off his angel wings? He hop back into their car with his posse and drive off, a line of car exhaust trailing them. And that was that.

II

THE REPENTERS

'It damn well felt illegal at the time, though.'

★

I make a promise to myself – I wasn't gon live on no pavement. So I was in and out of shelters after that. When they couldn't accommodate me, I went back to square one – sleepin in the library. But they decide to up their security and it wasn't long till they figure out my scheme and I end up gettin throw the hell out. But not before I spring a copy of *The Little Prince*. Kept it on me all the time, re-read it almost every night.

Sometimes I'd stay in them seedy, ramshackle guest houses. Stay for a while and the moans from behind the paper-thin walls won't bother you. Just background noise. Bosses and their secretaries, underaged girlfriends, bullermen tryin to grab a quick fuck before they go home to their wives. Your brain filters it out.

The rooms was cheap, but the savings was running out fast. Wasn't much to do in them guest houses except try to adjust to the present – enough to regret the past. I ain't gon lie. I went mad every once in a while. Use to beat up the bathroom. But most days I was in a dream state. Couldn't tell what day was what. Sometimes I'd just strip down, leave the shower runnin and sit under it. Never know when next I'd see one. It was the only time I could separate myself from the world. I let the water drown out everything. The rest of the world couldn't get me in there, even if just for a few minutes.

But I couldn't escape St. Asteria. It always come creepin back into my mind. St. Asteria and Mouse. Sometimes I wondered how different things woulda turn out if she didn't leave. Try to tell myself there ain't no point in speculatin. Ain't no proper comparisons to be made. Reach a minute early, reach a minute late, you never know what difference it could make. But somethin dawn on me, nevertheless. It ain't worth it to distance yourself from the people you grow up round. When you're alone, you feel that you don't exist, that if you die, nobody will know who you are.

I find comfort in rereading *The Little Prince* and rediscoverin how I felt when she was there. I think I finally understood. The lamplighter's problem was that he was alone. Humans ain't tailored to live alone. We might spend half the time killin each other or runnin from each other, but bein alone is never right. How could a man live on a planet by himself and not go mad? All he had was his duties. If he stopped lightin the lamp, he woulda have nothin else. He had to busy himself to keep the emptiness from gettin him. Trust me, you ain't know bout emptiness till you have nobody left in the world.

But how could I face people? It was shame all over again, just like with Bronson. I was damaged. I let Sanskrit damage me bad, even if I couldn't feel out the wounds. Was the type of injury that only look bad in some fancy X-ray. You can't feel the pain, but deep down, it's there. Sometimes I convince myself that that night was a nightmare. I'm waking up, I tell myself, I have to take it as it comes. I have to reach out. It was the only way.

Some of the guest houses had a phonebook at the front. One day, I flipped right to R. Ran my fingers down the names, lookin for one in particular: Romany. Surprising how many people was name Romany in Trinidad. There was no Maya Romany, but I remembered where she live, just from a passin mention from a moment we shared in the park opposite the parish back at St. Asteria. Sun Canyon Road with the yellow poui trees.

Yes, there was a listing in Sun Canyon Road. Matthew Romany. Her father? She woulda been in her mid twenties by then. Wasn't strange for her to be living at home at that age. Only marriage could separate some daughters from their parents. I scribbled the number at the back of *The Little Prince*, but I didn't call right away. It was terrifying. Even after Sanskrit, I wasn't sure I could pull through with this one and come out in one piece.

But one morning, I mustered the courage to shamble down to the payphone. I steadied my fingers and dialled the number. My heart was beatin fast-fast. As the phone rang, I thought bout what I was goin to say. Someone picked up. A man's voice. I asked to speak with Maya. He just say, 'Who's this?'

Didn't know what to say. I stammer out, 'Just an old friend.'

He hesitate, but then tell me to hold on. There was a minute of silence, which feel like an hour. I coulda hear chatterin in the background, and a parrot squawkin. Then I heard the phone pick up. A voice spoke. It was her.

When I told her who it was, she didn't say nothin at first. Then she murmur, 'Oh God.' And I can remember the way her tongue faltered on God and how her voice lingered on that word for so long.

I thought she woulda hang up, but she didn't. I told her I couldn't talk for long – which was true – and that we should meet up. Her voice was slow then – not cautious, but reluctant. I didn't expect anything else. I wasn't sure what I was doin or what we was gon talk bout when we see each other eye to eye.

A miracle happen. She say that she could meet me that evening at the TGIF near the savannah roundabout at six. I found my ass there at five. When I got there, she was already waiting. At least, I thought it was her. She was wearin an orange-and-white chequered shirt and a pair of navy blue jeans. Her hair was short, cut above her shoulders, styled into waves. She was fashionable. But there was other things different bout her. I focused on her face as she purse her lips and scanned the room. She looked sleepy. Jaded. Her collarbones look like they coulda collect water. Her face remind me how much people change with time.

She didn't see me. She sat near the hedges and lit up a cigarette. She take a long drag, watchin the joggers make their rounds on the savannah. I remained in the waiting area.

The frontwoman ask me bout three times if I'd like to be seated. I was worried it woulda draw attention, but nobody notice. Gal probably thought someone stand me up for a date. When Mouse finally come in, I keep my eyes on the floor, though I could feel the frontwoman's gaze on me at the same time.

She sat at the bar and ordered a drink. Somethin hard, probably. When I finally went up to her, she played it down. No hugs. No contact. Just restrained looks and awkward nods. A smile struggled to crack through her strawberry lipstick. A fake one. But that's okay. I am the man to know bout fake smiles – and the last to be offended by them.

She spoke with the drink in her hand, swishin the ice round. She had it there so her hands wouldn't fidget and stray. Then she let out, 'Jesus, Jordon. How old are you now?'

I tell her the truth. 'Eighteen.'

She raised her eyebrows, taking another sip. 'So you have the rest of your life ahead of you.'

I shrugged. 'Don't know what you mean by that. Life in motion for a long time now.'

'I went through a lot at your age too. Thought I could change the world.' She finished her drink and ordered another.

'In a sense, you did… a little.' I hunched over. 'For a while.'

She sat silent, glancing over at the waitress. Then she say, 'That's good to hear. Can't lie when I say St. Asteria just seem like a dream now.' She didn't continue until the waitress bring her drink. She take a sip.

'You know, being a sister had its advantages. Never had to pay a bus fare. They'd always refuse my money. It's a noble lifestyle. I really do love God and there was something romantic about wearing the veil.'

'That's why you ditch us?'

'I ditched – damn it, I hate usin that word – I left the convent, Jordon, not you. It was hard. People thought I left for a life of sex and sin. Truth is, being a nun just puts you in for a life of foolhardy obedience. I had to leave.'

She finished her second drink and ordered a third. She continued, 'I'd break down in the night. I heard about nuns leaving when they were forty. They'd wait all those years to leave just so it wouldn't look bad. It'd look like they paid their dues. I couldn't do it. I called up the Mother Superior, and I broke down again. When I finally had the courage to go back and look her in the face, she gave me the papers to sign and left the room. From her reaction, I could tell that I wasn't the first. That gave me some relief.'

'So you just had to sign?'

She took a sip and nodded. 'There wasn't any legal binding. It only took a month to go through. But I didn't have to wait for approval.' She slumped, going quiet for a while. 'It damn well felt illegal at the time, though. Maybe because it was so easy.'

She downed the drink and called for another. Then she said,

'You might think you are finished with the past. But the past ain't finished with you. You know what I mean, Jordon?'

'Yeah, I know what you – '

'I was so young and hasty back then. I hope God will forgive my hasty impulses. It seem a long time ago and only a few people know about those few St. Asteria years –' Her lips quiver. 'On my resumé, there is no mention of St. Asteria anywhere. I was wondering last night… Why would I leave that out? Why would I keep it a secret? Was it so shameful?'

She stopped herself to take another sip. 'It make me wonder what kinda person would think to lie about somethin like that?' She looked straight at me. 'Did they talk about me after I left?' She was beginning to slur.

Before I had the chance to answer, she shoot out, 'You forgive me, right?'

'It ain't have nothin to forgive – '

'I was so young when I joined. I was just a girl, just out of secondary school. Just halfway finished with my degree. I just wanted to help children. Wanted to give back and do a good thing. But when I got there, the conditions were so awful. It was so much worse than I thought it would be, Jordon.'

An old feelin wash over me as I remembered how I once wanted to sleep in and live in Mouse's room in St. Asteria, despite the dull brownness of it. Despite the mouldy, musty air floatin around the cobweb drapes. The old paint on the corners every mornin waitin to be swept out. Cockroaches waiting to be crunched with brooms. We tried our best to spruce it up, but in the end, the room still end up lookin like a cancer was eatin it away.

I say, 'We try to make it the best –'

'I didn't think,' she cut in. 'When I wanted to leave, I realize it wasn't even second thoughts. It was first thoughts! I wasn't thinking. One day I just woke up and thought I heard a calling. I told my Dad not to laugh at me.'

She put her head on the table. 'I don't know what compelled me to think it wouldn't be as hard as it was. But I stuck around and that has to count for somethin, right?'

'Right.' The word come out in a breath.

She glance at me. 'But you seem good now. Looks like you

made it out in one piece. I can't say the same for a lot of people that I know. I just hope that I added something to your life. All your lives. Even though I always try to forget about it. You understand why I try to forget about it, right?'

I tell her, 'When you were there, you made a lot of us happy. As I say, ain't have nothin to forgive.'

I then excuse myself to go to the toilet. I sat in there for about five minutes. Just remembering sitting with her on the couch in the study. Sitting on the step just to hear her sing in the shower. I was suddenly overcome with a deepening grief.

It hit me worse than the day she left St. Asteria. I don't know what I was expectin. A revelation? Maybe she coulda help me – I don't know why I thought she would want to. She had long move on from St. Asteria. I was lyin when I say it ain't have nothin to forgive. An act of betrayal is somethin that shouldn't easily be forgiven. Look like she's livin with it. Told you before, the bruises in the mind don't heal easily, and there's always somethin that gon prod against it. I knew I was that somethin, the tongue probing the sore, the itch under the scab. I had no interest in having that kinda relationship with anybody.

The Mouse I knew ain't that woman sittin over at the bar. I ain't know why I was fixin to convince myself otherwise. Sometimes people don't add up to be what you want them to be.

I wait until the bathroom was empty before I come out the cubicle. I look at my haggard image in the mirror as I wash my hands and wet my face.

When I come out the bathroom, Mouse had her head on the table still. Drunk. I had probably never cross her mind before that night, and maybe it was best that way.

I make a run for it.

The frontwoman call out to me as I make a quick lunge out the door. I didn't hear what she say. I was already gone, already across the road, already hit the pavement, lost somewhere along the joggers and runners that was making their rounds around the savannah.

'We've become too dependent on God.'

★

There was just one place I had left. All the way back south. Back to St. Asteria. It was frightenin to go back – even more frightenin to think that I couldn't stay. I needed a place to live, not just endure. I needed a place to heal.

There were floods the morning I got there, so I couldn't go in right away. The rain come down like no other that year. A pall of iron-grey cloud draggle cross the sky.

I shelter under the small gazebo at the centre of the park. I traced my fingers along its chipped wooden balusters, some of them snap off. A used condom lie tucked away between two of the wooden posts. A trio of beer bottles stood on the railing. The walls was strewn with graffiti obscenities and the spraypainted names of girls. Termites had made their home along the wooden crenellations that lined the top, and the weather vane wasn't there no more and nobody trouble to replace it.

Castle Grayskull had fallen.

Withered leaves carpeted two of the walkways that radiated from the gazebo. It had two other walkways, where the almond trees was reduced to sad stumps, decapitated. Maybe hit by some pest or plague. Each time the thunder crack out, I felt like there would be some sinkhole in the earth that would swallow me. I couldn't see another soul. Out on the grass, a plastic bag swivel madly in the wind, twistin up to the sky and circlin back to the ground.

Hell, I coulda barely see the house, the words painted in a clumsy arc over the gate: St. Asteria Home for Children. A fragment of the parish poke out in the background, triangular and jagged, the stubbled lawn ending clean and clear along the overflowing runnels. The building was postcard-pretty amongst its company of dilapidated houses, occupied, but unmaintained by their inhabitants. Corrugated iron roofs shaking with the rain, sounds like coins fallin into a steel drum.

The drains was spilling over, the roads now like rivers. Between me and the house lay this murky ocean. My final option, only a few breaststrokes away.

The rain wasn't gon stop, so I decide to make a run for it. Not to the house, but to the parish at the back. The same one where we prayed for salvation every Sunday, where I lock eyes with Jesus as I hear how Mr. and Mrs. Sant meet their demise.

I dash through the water and under the arch to the parish entrance. It was the same: the hedges of ixoras and bougainvillea lining the walkway, the guttering pipes dripping and leaking into the barrels below, the vineyard of barbwire curling along the walls. I take a moment to breathe in the memories before I went inside.

I sat on the pew, slippin outta my soggy shoes. The familiar smell of wood shavings hit me straight away. I inhale it, absorb it in my lungs and blood. I notice a figure at the altar. An old man dress in black. I knew who it was straight away. The thick glasses, skin like a coalpot, beard like chalk. He come up to me, taking slow steps. I try not to look at him. But he was looming over me now and I had no choice.

'Just come here to shelter from the rain, son?'

As I look up at him, his whole face went slack. Then he mutter, '*Oh fuuu…*'

He sat on the pew on the other side of the aisle, lookin like he woulda topple over if he hadn't sat down. His eyes linger on me, his jaw muscles bulging, chin jutting out.

'Father,' I say. 'You ain't age a day.'

He didn't say my name. He sat silent, his legs sprawling forward on the aisle, still beset by this phantom before him. But he didn't remain so for long. He gather himself, loosening his sleeves and tightening his jaw. Then he just quip, 'It's all the wine.'

I come right out with it. 'Father, I need a place to stay.' When he didn't reply, I add in, 'Just for now.'

He nodded. He looked me straight in the eye, probably to see if I was high on anything. I suspected it was a commonplace thing to have ruined children come back with similar wishes. Was I ruined. I hoped not. Coloured-outta-the-lines, perhaps.

He said, 'Since Sister Maura passed, things haven't been easy here.'

'Sister Mother died? When?' I lean forward, arms across my kneecaps.

'Not too long after you were gone. She was dying for a while. Diabetic – bet you didn't know that. Also bet you didn't know she couldn't see. Not blind, but very nearly so.'

'Since when?'

'For years, boy.'

'How the others take it?'

'Her passing? They took it as it came. It hit me hard – but I'm a man like that. We buried her in the parish. Sister Bernice – what was it you all used to call her –'

'Bulldog.'

He chuckle, almost snorting. 'Sister Bernice transferred out. She's doing well.'

'So, who's left?'

Father Anton point to himself. Then he say, 'From who you know? The only one left is Ti-Marie. She helps out with the children. We have volunteers from time to time, but Ti-Marie is the only regular.'

Faces flash through my head as he began to rattle off, 'Jerrick does some work offshore – he's in training. He did well for himself. I'd like to think I played some part in that. Can't speak for Quenton. Jeannine left bout a year ago. She met some boy, got pregnant by him. I ain't never met him, but she lives with him and his mother now. Same happened with Rey. Met some girl and he moved in with them. Who am I missing?'

'Pinky – Marissa Kelly?'

'Her father showed up some years back, out of the blue. He took her in. I haven't heard from her since.'

'Sookie?'

'Right, right. Sookie used to come back to help out. Haven't seen her in about a year, though. She probably got the happiest ending of all – lives in a gated community in the West with a couple who came up to St. Asteria one day. Don't know how long they kept it in their heads or if they made the decision on a whim. But they walked right up to St. Asteria one day with one Biblical passage in mind: James 1:27.'

'What does that say?'

'*Religion that God our Father accepts as pure and faultless is this: to look after orphans and widows in their distress.*' He just sat there nodding. 'But they couldn't just take her like that. She had to give permission. It was sad, but I helped speed the process up. Them being rich white folk also helped speed it up. God was watching over that girl, I could tell you that.'

'What bout the rest of us? God watchin over us, you think?'

'Hard to say.' He turn to look at the giant crucifix over the altar. 'I had a sermon two Sundays back, bout this here self. We've become too dependent on God. We have to look out for each other now, I think. Everybody needs their own protector. Every man jack that walk this Earth is a sinner. God favours some of them, gives them the opportunity to drag themselves outta it. They repent and escape damnation. But what about the rest of us repenters?'

'You think we're all repenting?'

'Son, as soon as we cross the age of accountability, that is all we are – repenters, for our own sins and for the sins of those who came before us. The only way to repent is to make it easier for your fellow man to survive, and repent his own sins. Pull him up through the mire so he can be forgiven. If you know God watches over you, you have a responsibility to watch over others as well.'

'You'd say God watches over you, Father?'

'I think He does, yes. And I think He's fine with the life I've been living, but not so satisfied with some of the decisions I've made.'

'Like what?'

I coulda hear him swallow.

'Sister Katherine?'

'She shoulda been front page news that day. That wasn't no kinda thing to sweep under the rug.'

He paused. The rain was quieting outside. 'I didn't blame you when you left. I can't pretend to imagine how you felt – knowing she was still out there. But I know it shattered your trust in us.'

I lifted my eyes to look at him. Then I give him a small nod. I let him believe what he wanted to believe. Let him fill in his own blanks with his own guilt.

'I want to do right by you, Jordon,' he say.

I knew I had him. 'Father, I have nowhere to live.'

'You're on the street?'

'In and out. I have no place to call home. Never had, except St. Asteria. I was wondering –'

'Are you in any trouble?'

'Like, if police are lookin for me?'

'Any type of trouble.'

He was digging to find the wounds, the broken wings, the rabies blood. I couldn't blame him, but I couldn't let him quarantine me. He couldn't know what I went through, no. Let it come later, I thought. Let me through the doors now. I will repay the debts. I had to clench my jaw, breathe easy, slow my heartbeat. So I just tell him, as convincing as I could, 'I lost my job and I can't pay my rent. That's the trouble, Father.'

'I can set a space for you here.' He turn to look at the crucifix. 'You need clothes?'

'I have clothes. But I can always do with extra.'

'It won't be free. You'll have to work.'

'What do I have to do?'

'I'd like you to help out with the children. Think you can handle that?'

Yes, people do anything to save themselves, especially if they're the grievin kind. I've just been fortunate to be around during their times of grief. These repenters – make them your best friends. Keep them close. And if you're one yourself, don't save each and everybody. Not everybody is ready to be saved.

'Me?'

My eyes are open.

'Can't help but feel a lil jealous.'

★

Father Anton brought me to his rectory and let me shower there. On the bed was a disarray of clothes – old donations from the Sunday people. I had my pick. I stood in the middle of the bedroom, in the rinse of the bright yellow light, feeling cleansed. I wiggled my toes against the soft carpet, absorbing the texture against the soles of my feet. Plastic decorations dangled from the ceiling, made from the undersides of plastic bottles, cut to look like waxflowers and strung together with twine.

The sky was clearing up, the wind now lapping against a pair of tall ferns I could see through the slit of the curtains. I shut the curtains and slip the towel off. Careful, I lay on the bed. I felt like a nestling wrapped in its mother's glossy feathers. I was shivering in anticipation of a new life and flinching from the resurgence of the old.

I put on my clothes. They was a bit tight, but they were only temporary. As I come out the room, I see Father Anton sittin opposite a girl at a table in the kitchen. She was leaning forward, facing him, her arms on the table. Her cleavage burst from her tank top, which was a size too small – a reminder that Sister Mother was indeed dead – a sight she would not have permitted. She didn't have the bantu knots no more. Her hair was now in tight, neat shoulder-length braids, some of them jet black, some of them dyed bronze-brown.

As she turn to me, her lips parted. Father Anton didn't say nothin – he let the revelation sink in. She then turn to him and back to me, slowly rising from the chair. 'This can't be real,' she say, blinking at me, that familiar smile lingering on her lips. She turn to Father Anton and ask, 'This for real?'

'Ti-Marie,' he say, 'Jordon Sant, in the flesh.'

She threw her arms round me, pat my back and whisper, 'God is good, boy.' She look at me, her arms still grippin onto me. Her grin made me feel like she was gon kiss me. Her body had fill out, but her face was exactly the same. When she let go, she ask, excited like a child, 'You stickin round then?'

'As long as Father lets me,' I tell her.

'You should meet the children,' Father Anton say, gettin up from the chair.

They tell me to relax till it was time. My mind reel back to the days when we get a new addition to St. Asteria. Sister Mother woulda clap her hands and holler out, 'Important announcement! This concerns everybody!' and we'd line up, side to side, for the introduction.

I wondered what Ti-Marie was gonna say bout me. Even I wouldn't know what to say bout me.

When it was time, the three of us walk across to the main residence. The grass crunched beneath my feet, reminding me of how we use to line up and march along this same path for Sunday mass and choir practice. My stomach was grumbling, the acidic pang of nervousness setting in, but nothin enough to weaken me. Just felt like a motor gently chuggin in my guts. Had no choice but to roll with it.

Takin that first step back into the St. Asteria residence really set the weight down, boy. It seize me by the hipbones. I coulda fall over – was too much. The place ain't change. The walls was repainted, but in the same manner that give it that look of yellowed glassine paper. Everything was preserved, from the same featherdrilled holes near the lintels of the windows, to the old cracked ceramics on the counters. The only addition was a framed portrait of Sister Mother, blown up a little too big, hanging on the wall alongside the staircase.

At the foot of the steps, the children – three boys and four girls – was gathered, impatiently awaiting the introduction. I clench my teeth hard. I couldn't look any of them in the eye. It was harder than I thought being on the other side of things.

'Ladies and gentlemen of St. Asteria,' Ti-Marie start off. 'I would like to introduce you to the new addition to our staff. This is Mr. Jordon. Mr. Jordon lived here, just like you, for most of his life. He has recently decided to come back to help out. The Lord has brought him to us and we are very grateful to have him here.'

She looked at me and smiled.

Then they utter in unison, 'The St. Asteria family welcomes you, Mr. Jordon.'

Then I just stood there. Rabbit in the headlights. Everybody expecting me to say somethin, but nothin coming to mind. So I just give a bow and smile. Ti-Marie cut in, her glance jumpin between me and the children, 'I just want to add something. I grew up with Mr. Jordon. Right in this house. We know it ain't easy – yes, believe me, we know. We went through some hard times – still goin through it. But me and him know how it is. It is a blessing to have him here.' She then turn to me and repeat, 'A real blessing.'

Ti-Marie then led me up the stairs. The first door, Mouse's room, was not only shut tight, but the doorknob was missin. I guess they never bother to replace it. It had nothin behind there for me, though seein it touch me with sadness.

Ti-Marie point me to a door – Sister Bulldog's old room. 'Your room,' she tell me. She then point to the one opposite. 'And mine.'

'You sleepin in Sister Mother's room?'

'I rotate. I's the only one who living up here, you know. Till now.'

'Dunno how I feel bout sleepin in old Bulldog's bed,' I say, chuckling.

'Aye. You ain't ever even taste the tambran – what you worry-ing bout? Have no nightmares for you.'

'Always a first time for everything, you know.'

I spent most of the day just observing the children, and I learn quick how different things was. Even though the shell of St. Asteria was preserved, the blood flowin through it was of a different creature. I ain't shame to say that the new inhabitants of St. Asteria was better than us.

They moved as a unit, more coordinated, more willing. Better-behaved, smarter, more talented. They had to be. Nobody was cleanin up for them anymore, like how the nuns woulda give us a hand from time to time. Doin the laundry, scrubbing the shower was punishment for us – not necessary labour. These children already knew how to prepare their own food, and I ain't talkin bout bread and butter and Mac and cheese. The younger ones sliced the vegetables, and the older ones seasoned meat and operated the stove. There was no Rico and Quenton to fuck up the amity. There was no need for no Bulldog and no tambran whip.

When it was time to sleep, they didn't fight and cuss for top bunk and bottom bunk. Not like we did. There was no time for small-mindedness. Stinginess was outta the question. Was like they had an understanding of their place in the world and their own winding, miry roads. They already learn the fact that if God wasn't watchin over you, you had to look out for each other.

At the end of the day, just after lights out downstairs, I follow Ti-Marie to the back of the parish. There, she fix her eyes on a cross-shaped gravestone, already weathered grey, its base enmeshed in a knotted wheel of moss and elephant grass. On it was chiselled our matriarch's name:

SISTER MAURA EDITH MCCONELL
Survived by all her children at St. Asteria.

Ti-Marie prop up her legs against her chest, the breeze ruffling the edge of her long skirt.

'You feel sad on the day she die?' I ask her.

'More scared than sad.'

'What bout now? How you feel?'

She purse her lips. 'I wish she was here sometimes.'

'You liked her so much?'

'She use to hold everything together.'

I shrugged. 'Things seem to be holdin together good here from what I see.'

'Yeah?'

'Yeah. You doin a good job.'

She give me a smile. I woulda thought she'd be prattlin non-stop after all these years, but all we could share was silence. But it was comfortable silence. When we went back to the house, Ti-Marie head to the kitchen and ask me to reach the top shelf for a jar of peanut butter. A drawing of a skull-and-crossbones was taped to it. When I handed it to her, she dug out a chunk of it and spread it over a slice of wheat bread.

I say, 'You have to fill me in here.'

'It have rat poison in it.'

'For what?'

She chuckle, still spreading the toxic mixture. 'For the rats.'

'Peanut butter?' I say.

She set the bread on an old, cracked saucer. 'Work better than cheese, believe me.' She put the saucer on the floor, and I put the jar back where I found it.

When we went up to our rooms, it finally set in – panic. I had slept in so many unfamiliar rooms, so many dingy shitholes. Now, I was in paradise, and I wanted to piss my pants. I was overwhelmed, afraid to be alone here in the nuns' quarters, staying here, after they abandon it. I dunno why, but it feel like I was sleepin in one of them old leper houses up in Chacachacare.

Ti-Marie was in the bathroom, an old white nightie draping her body. A row of tiny moles lined the side of her collar. I sat on the toilet lid and watched her brush her teeth. She glance at me through the mirror and say, 'Is different, eh? Seein it from this angle.'

'Everything's different. The same, but different.'

'Boy, that is what growin up feel like.' She spit. 'Is scary, getting old.'

'We ain't old.'

'If you ain't a child, you old – trust me. Once you cross sixteen, you old. World treat you different from then on.'

I steeple my fingers on my chin, rememberin all the people who use to walk past me on the street. I say, 'World moves forward and forgets you.'

'Let it forget me then. I fraid the world, boy.' She spit. 'This world ain't for me.'

'What you mean?'

'Sympathy is only for the young. As for the rest – the rest of we is of little value. We don't even see others as fellow human beings. That's why nobody trust each other. You only trust the people you grow up with as a child.'

'So, you trust me then?'

She spit one last time and start rinsing her mouth. 'We come from the same place. I ain't even gon bother ask what happen during them years you was gone, because to me, it ain't matter.'

My mind flash back to the bullet in Sanskrit's skull. 'It ain't matter?'

'What matter is that you end up back here.'

'That is why you say what you say bout family?'

She look at me through the mirror. 'What I say?'

'Family is who you choose to be with.'

She turn to look at me. 'So, you understand where I comin from. You come back to the place where you ain't have to assume the worst in everybody. Right?'

'I guess so, yeah. Life gon be easier here.'

'How come you remember what I say?'

I chuckle, 'Girl, I remember what stick with me. A sentence here and there. Things I pick up – everything have meaning in the end. But most of all, I guess I remember things that turn out to be true.'

'What else you remember?'

'We have nothin to give each other but weselves.'

'Amen,' she say, smiling.

'How you feel bein round these children?'

She take a seat next to me on the toilet lid – our hips touching. She shrug and say, 'Can't help but feel a lil jealous.'

'Me too.'

She smile, nudging me with her shoulder. 'They help each other. Is sad to look at them and remember our own time here, and realize how much all of we did struggle to live with each other.'

'We was sour children.'

She slap my shoulder. 'Mister, I was always sweet as a plum! I dunno what you talkin bout!'

When she got up, the panic set in again.

When I got into bed, it swallow me, it was so big. The blanket was thick and fluffy. I ball it up in a thick bundle and wrap my arms round it. Only the smooth whir of the fan to keep me company. Couldn't sleep. I swear, I sleep better in sheets stinkin of diesel and stain with semen, where the mosquitoes come and go as they please, and centipedes would crawl down the bedpost

149

and under the pillow. I didn't feel like me anymore. Not with these ironed clothes, clipped fingernails and shampooed hair.

I went back out to the hall. Lingered outside Ti-Marie's door, wondering if to knock. I drag my knuckles down the wood of the door, along the hasps. Then I just give it a light tap-tap-tap.

'Ti-Marie,' I say, and she open the door.

'Can't sleep?' she say. 'You probably have plenty on your mind.'

She motion me to come in. As I did, the first thing I see was a relic of the past, scotch-tape to a wall right beside the closet. My drawing. Tears on sand, sprouting roses, colour pencil and graphite – my recreation of Ti-Marie's dream. All these years, the paper old and crumpled, but still intact. My name in chickenfoot in the corner.

She play it down, didn't want to make a big deal outta it. She sat on the edge of the bed, saying, 'Couldn't sleep the first night I had to come upstairs to live. I ain't even gon pretend to know how much worse it must be for you.'

At that moment, I burst into tears. All the shit I went through, and I ain't cry since I ain't know when. Back when I was alone in them guesthouses, I used to kick the wall, hammer my fists against the pillow, knock my head against the bathroom tiles, dip my head in the filled sink and scream into it. It was never like this. Not tears like these. I didn't feel shame to cry in front of Ti-Marie.

It feel… good.

She pull me into her arms, slipping one of her palms under the back of my shirt. She trail her fingertip down my spine as she shush me. Here was this girl, a full year younger than me, playin mother for me. 'Sleep here tonight,' she say, her jaw resting on the crook of my shoulder.

When I had calm down, I went to the bathroom and slosh my face with water. She wipe her thumb down from my eye, swabbing a bit of salt off from my cheek. We didn't say anything when we come back to the room. We close the door, switch off the lights. She lie on her side and pull me against her, tucking the curve of her fiddle-shaped back against my chest, her braids under my chin, her butt proddin against my groin. I listened to her breathing – almost like soft coos.

Accustomed to the darkness, my eyes flitted round, mapping

out the room. It was almost identical to Bulldog's, but there was no drapes on the window. Instead, a row of Venetian blinds lay askew, siftin through a few slats of moonlight. The cool air that eddy in was gentle, carrying with it a faint, diffused smell that remind me of brewing coffee. Ti-Marie lean closer against me and whisper, 'You cold?'

'I'm okay.'

There was a pause as she shuffle under me. Her voice was frail, cracking. 'You know, you should stay. Live right here.'

'I'm not goin anywhere.'

She turn to me and I don't know who do it first. I think is one of them moments where nobody is to blame. There wasn't no words. Just breaths. Our lips touched. I dunno bout her, but that was my first kiss. We break outta formation and scrambled to find a position that suit us best.

'This your first time?' she whisper to me.

'Yeah.'

'Good.'

'You?'

'Yes.'

I slick some spit on my dick, though I didn't need to. She was way past ready, probably even before the kiss. She kept her nightie on at first – she had it hike up to her belly. And we made no noise – tried our best not to. The bed squeak and creak, but that was it. There was nobody else upstairs to hear us. There was no technique or method. I didn't know what I was doin, and she didn't neither. I went according to her breaths, usin it as a meter of sorts. It wasn't violent or gentle. But it wasn't just physical. I don't know what it was. It wasn't love – not in the romantic sense, or what star-crossed lovers feel during some rare reunion. No, nothin like that.

We didn't talk, even after it was done. Only when we was done, she take off her nightie. We just lie there, pasted with sweat, still overcome by what happen – and that was how it feel, yes, like something happen to us. Like it wasn't our actions. Like it was external. And we know it was the right thing.

She know it and I know it.

And right as we prep ourselves to go the second time, she put her hand on my cheek and say, 'Let's make it last.'

'Somebody need to take care of that dog.'

★

We fall asleep after the second time. I push myself against her backside and was flat out in two minutes. I was sleepin good until a clattering wake me up, like knuckles rapping on galvanize, but then quickly morphing into a clanging, like a metal chain jangling against concrete. It was loud. It coulda wake up the whole building.

When I wake up I was in a panic. Like I was fallin, my body flailin in the roll of the dark sky, no sound but the wind. That waking dread again. But I had a strange notion this time – one I never feel before. Roll to my side and see Ti-Marie next to me, the nape of her neck near my mouth, and I reap the fear that she would suddenly think this whole thing was a mistake. I was deathly afraid of bein rejected, that she would push me aside, haul two big chains over her chest and slap a padlock over her heart.

I wasn't in love. At least, I don't think so. I ain't never been in love, so how would I know, anyhow? The only explanation I ever get for how it feel is that I would know when the time come. I wasn't in any kinda love. It was obsession all over again, just like with Mouse. But I was older now and this was different. Was a restrained craze, feelin like someone else's body belong to you. You could caress it, undress it, squeeze it between your fingers, dig your nails into it, bite it. Be close to it. Similarly, you'd let that person do the same. You'd trust them with your body, even though they might tie you up and beat you with a cord. Maybe this is the fruit of loneliness. You cut your skin a little everytime you want to let someone in. Bleedin for someone is no easy task.

I put my hand over her ass and she shifted closer to me. Maybe she was lonely too. Maybe the circumstances was just right. Maybe havin somethin good was hard to believe when most of your life you're accustom to choosin between bad and worse. You scrutinize every good thing until either they get tired of you, or you get tired of them.

When the clatterin start back up, it almost jolt me right outta the bed. Ti-Marie turn to watch me. She didn't say nothin at first. I wasn't even sure if she was awake.

'What the hell is that noise?' I ask.

'Is just Chopper,' she reply, in a groaning, sleep-clogged voice. 'You remember Chopper.'

'Chopper? Chopper still livin?'

'Somebody need to take care of that dog.'

I hop outta bed and put on my pants. I pull the blinds open and peek out, trying to trace the sound. I didn't have to look for long. Saw it almost straight away. The large lumbering figure, visible in the yard next door, thrustin itself against a stack of galvanize.

It really was Chopper.

So this was Granger's monster. I bet he beat it till he kill it, and then put it out in the thunderstorm and let the lightnin shock it back to life. This was the result of years of legions of little boys stamping their feet, hooting and hollerin, pushing a branch through the fence to poke the dog. Years of bloodstained beatings, years of bruises. Livin a life of confined pain would seem nothin but a fever dream. The idea of ownin a body fades away – it ain't yours anymore. It belong to the world instead, and the world will do with it what it pleases.

I remember thinkin – Fuck, this coulda be me.

The only thing that separate the beast from its yard and the street was a few slats of wood. It started to drizzle. Didn't hear it, but saw it under the streetlamps. Rain drifting gently in the light. The beast still thrashing against its chain. The lights flick on in Granger's house and I see him trampling down the outside stairs – bareback, a dark thatch of hair under his belly. He make his way down to the dog, steel pipe in hand. He lift it and swing it, bringing it upon the dog's back. The dog let out a yelp and a howl before stooping and lying on its side, suddenly calm. Its ribs heaving. Up and down. Up and down. My mind shoot back to some old primary school teachers who use to say, 'We have to beat all of you like dog before you listen!'

'What goin on down there?' Ti-Marie ask, on the verge of driftin back to sleep.

'So look like Granger still around?' I say, keeping my eyes on Granger as he waddle back up the stairs and slam the door.

'Unfortunately,' she say. I watched for a few more minutes. When my eyes cut back to her, she was asleep.

The next two nights I wake up in a panic again. Cold sweating. The dog goin crazy. Waking up like that, it's thoughts about death that blindside you. This was it. This was the wounds finally rippin open.

Both nights, I spring outta bed and pull the blinds to watch the dog. Ti-Marie wake up in the middle of the madness and ask sleepily, 'You all right, Jordon?' before falling back asleep.

The next night, she sit up in bed, rubbing her eyes. 'Jordon? You all right?'

'We coulda stop him, you know,' I say. 'Granger.'

'Remember how much police visits he had? His wife never want to press charges. Have nothin we coulda do.'

'No, I mean – at least back then we coulda save the dog. Why we didn't save the dog?'

'You crazy? How?'

'We coulda scale the wall. Untie the leash and set it free.'

'And get your tail blaze with tambran from Bulldog when we get catch? What kinda plan is that?'

I shrug. 'You don't think the dog could hurt somebody?'

'That poor dog never leave the yard in he whole dismal life. The only danger that dog pose is to the man, Granger, heself. And rightly so if it ever happen.'

'You say somebody need to take care of that dog. Why not me and you?'

'You all right, Jordon?'

I close the blinds. 'Tambran is nothin compare to what that dog went through.'

'Where all this comin from?' She get up from the bed and hug me from behind. I shudder and nearly push her off. But instead, I turn and close my eyes and sink into her. It was better than the sex. We just lie in bed and she kept huggin me. At that moment, I felt drunk. Perhaps that was the intention. Get drunk and tell the

154

truth. She deserved the truth. Not the whole truth. Not even I know the whole truth about the Carnival Tuesday, so I left that out. Only God can judge me on that. But I told her everything else.

When I was done, she just look at me, her eyes warm and misty, and put her palm on my face. 'I'm glad you can talk to me,' she said. 'And I'm glad you're safe.'

17

'This is me being brave.'

★

I saw these children as parts of a functioning machine. Each one a cog, a well-oiled joint, a bolt carefully fastened. Each one with a purpose in St. Asteria, and a purpose in the world. Might sound bad to say this, but it was difficult to see them as individuals when they operated so much like, well, machine parts. Sister Mother, whenever we did stupid things, use to shake her head and just quip, 'You play stupid games, you win stupid prizes.'

I wondered how she would have felt bein round these children. Maybe happy. Perhaps she died happy.

There was one child who cast herself aside. It ain't surprising that it was this child who catch my eye, this one stand-out who couldn't fit herself into the apparatus. This was Saleema Javed. Or Sal, as all the children call her. Sal was eight, and Sal was smart. She was ahead of her class. The school encourage her to skip a whole standard, so she was not only ahead, but she was also the youngest. She was smart in every sense, except for one: Sal wholeheartedly believed that her mother would come back for her.

Father Anton give me the story one afternoon. There was no calamity that bring Saleema to St. Asteria. Not no car crash, no gunshot, no Gramoxone. Not even no teenage pregnancy, or rape. Saleema was born to a thirty year-old woman who had all the facilities to raise her, but choose to give her up. She pass through Heavenly Anchorage for the first three years, and come to St. Asteria Home for Children just after. Woulda be right after I run away.

Father Anton try his best not to use the B word, but he still end up spillin it out, 'I don't see children as *burdens*. Ever. Children don't ask to be born.'

Sal never eat dinner with the other children. Just like when I was a child, the big old dining table was still in use. The family that eat together, stay together? Whatever. But we had to do it back when Sister Mother was the boss. We couldn't carry no food back to our room like it was take-out from a restaurant. No, no, no! That was a sin and a transgression.

But that was the only way Sal would have it. She was the only one allow to do this too, livin in the counterfeit world her mother forge. Sal's mother was only present in the postcards and letters she mailed from all over the world. It was the strangest case of child abandonment. It was like her mother was determine to be visible but perpetually out of reach.

Father Anton reluctantly admitted to me that he would read the mother's letters before givin them to Sal. There was nothing personal written in them. Just descriptions of trips, sometimes as impersonal as travel logs. Some of them even in third person. The back of the photos always had some cryptic caption.

The one on the summit overlooking Macchu Pichu: *Not all who wander are lost.*

Lying among a cluster of red crabs on Christmas Island: *Don't have to walk forward to get anywhere.*

Standing before the horns of bronze statue of a charging bull in New York: *This is me being brave.*

Sal use to wait heart in mouth for each one. She obsess over them, gluing and stapling each one into an old scrapbook. She save every envelope, every stamp, every return address. In between her study sessions, the girl just keep to her room, combing over the details. The other children never make it their business. There was talk of it, yes, but it was never directed at her.

When Father Anton tell me bout it, he jerk his finger up and down at me and say, 'Don't say anything to that girl about her mother. It's best she realizes for herself.'

'Realize what?'

'That her mother only does this to keep her own guilt at bay.'

'You think so?'

'Saleema's mother is a ghost. Rattles the cupboards at night. Rearranges fridge magnets to spell words. That's all she is.'

'So, you sayin she hauntin her daughter?'

157

'Jordon.' He put his hand on my shoulder. 'Anybody who wishes to communicate with you and gives you no way to say anything back to them – what else could that be but a haunting?' He shrug his shoulders. 'Maybe the woman will come back. And maybe cocks will grow teeth.'

By the time I come back to St. Asteria, Sal's mother hadn't written in a year. The girl spend all her time with her scrapbook, flipping through each letter, studying each photo caption. Cocking her head, her face resolute, searching for some clue, some sign between the words. Perhaps visiting these places in her mind. Swimming in Half Moon Cay, picking truffles in Holland, wading through snow in rural England.

Sal would go on the lone computer in St. Asteria. Only had dialup Internet back then – you know, when web pages took years to load. She moved from obsessing over the letters to her mother's blog. *A LiveJournal*, regularly updated. It only took entering her mother's name in a search engine to reveal this treasure trove.

There was no mention of a Saleema anywhere in the blog. That figured – why would there be? She never knew the girl. So what would she have to say about this unknowable little girl back in the Caribbean? It ain't take long to figure out in the past year that Sal's mother get married. But she stuck with her surname.

One day, Sal got sick. She had a blazing fever. The first two nights, me and Ti-Marie put her to sleep upstairs. It was normal for us to quarantine sick children like this at night. Also, the beds up there was bigger and more comfortable. They wouldn't have to fight to go to the bathroom. We massaged Vicks on the girl's chest and patted Limacol on her sweaty forehead. Ti-Marie stroke the girl's hair as if it was her own child.

The other children help out too – making soup, fashioning ice packs. But it got worse and Sal needed to go to the hospital. Father Anton drive her there and he wait the usual five hours just so a doctor could diagnose her with dengue, and say that she had to wait another five hours for a bed. Father Anton put up a fight, but the house always wins, eh.

He end up bringin her back here. The girl just needed two things: hydration and rest. It was our mission to make sure she could get it. The hydration wasn't no issue. But the girl couldn't rest – not with Granger's beast waking her up five times a night. Sal and I had that one thing in common. We both had night terrors, and it was because of that dog. The feelin was like we was being eaten alive, and we needed to spring outta the beast's mouth before it lock its jaw down on us. That was how Sal describe it, and I knew exactly what she was talking bout. I had a connection with this child, tellin you so.

Ti-Marie come to me one evening and say, 'Jordon, I see it now. What you said about Chopper.'

'How so?'

'I went to see that dog. I just stood outside the gate and watched. At first, I couldn't, but then I realize I never really watch the dog, not in a long time. Is one of them things I was avoiding. But you know what – you was right. We coulda do something.'

'It not too late. Have no tambran to cut we tail if we get catch.'

'*We?* What *we* gon do, Jordon?'

'We gon take care of the dog, just as you say.' I was surprise how easy the words come out.

She was quiet for a while, tracing her toes along the floor. She then nod and give me a quiet, 'Yeah.'

So we come up with a plan.

Late in the night, she went in the fridge, scouring for meat. Stew chicken – leftovers from dinner. She mash it up and got the rat poison from the cupboard. She slip it into the crushed meat and roll the whole thing up into a fat, gooey orb. Was bout the size of a cricket ball. She put it in a small plastic bag and give it to me.

I had to put on a raincoat, because a drizzle just started. I zip it up and pull the hood over my head, pick up a flashlight.

Just as I was bout to leave, she look at me. 'Maybe we shouldn't.'

'Granger not comin out in this weather,' I say.

She laugh. 'I only wish I coulda be so brave.'

I cross the street, peeking up at the windows of Granger house. Both still black out. The rain start to come down heavy. Chopper was howlin and rattlin the galvanize, even before he see me through the wire fence. I shine the light on him. He was growling at me from behind the gate. Lickin his own distended mouth. Leanin forward with his hackles up like spikes. Twistin the chain taut just to rear its head at me. I expect it to bare its teeth at me, to bound and hurtle towards me and choke itself, let the chain wring round its neck. But it just sit there, tremblin in the rain.

Chopper realize the outcome. It ain't fight it. I wave my hand in front of its face, revealing the ball of meat. At that moment, I feel sorry for the dog. I remember it as a puppy. I remember it tryin to shade under the middens of scrap metal. But that was then. This is now. It's too late and it have nothing worse than too late.

I wind up my arm, and I pitch the ball of meat right at the dog. It lap it up.

When the deed was done, my heart wanted to explode. I wanted to fall to my knees and scream out in the rain all of a sudden. As if I had slay some demon, some evil demigod. I scramble back to St. Asteria, nearly trippin over the pavement twice. Ti-Marie grab the coat off of me as soon as I swoop through the door. 'You do it? You do it?' she ask.

'We did it,' I say, a big grin on my face.

The next day, Granger come poundin the door, letting out a vile string of obscenities, blaming the children for the death of his dog, sayin he look out the window and see someone scamper from his yard right back here. He was demandin every child's head. He was threatenin to sue, shut down this society of dog-killers we was raisin. Ti-Marie swear that the man was gon take a cutlass to her, how stark raving mad he was.

'No child would even go near that dog,' she tell him. 'That dog was damn rabid and you damn well know that.'

He point at her face and she slap his hand away without missin a beat.

'I ain't your wife,' she say. 'Get it straight, mister. If you touch me, I ain't hesitatin to call the police on your ass. Nobody here never wanted anythin to do with your damn dog while he was alive. And we certainly ain't want nothin to do with the dog now he dead.' The children was huddled in the dining room, listenin. They had to bite their hands to keep from laughin out.

Even though the night panics disappear after that, I'd still wake up thinking about the dog – wonderin if we did the right thing. Sometimes I felt the urge to wake Ti-Marie so we could talk bout it. But then I realized that it wasn't important to ask that. Not when nobody in that dog's life did the right thing.

18

'I need you to be fearless now.'

★

Nobody else was home – just me and Sal. The rest of the children was at school, and Ti-Marie and Father Anton had gone for groceries. Groceries for St. Asteria was a whole other story, believe me. I stay back to take care of Sal. Dengue ain't no joke, but she was makin one outta it. Like me, she was sleeping sound after Chopper was gone. The fever and joint pains had subside, mostly. The vomiting had stop too. All that was left was a mild throbbing in her head and a twinge behind the eyes.

I was sittin on a chair beside the bed. I offer to read her something, but she just say, 'I don't like being read to. I like to read on my own.' She just lie in the bedroom upstairs – the one that had belong to Sister Mother – with the scrapbook in her lap, leafing through the postcards and photo.

'What's the last one you got?' I ask her.

She flip to the last page and show me. It was a photo of her mother smiling with a giant soapstone statue of Christ in the background, arms wide open, embracing the world. The photo was captioned: *Never forget who saved you and what you were saved from.*

I ask her, 'That's Jesus?'

'Christ the Redeemer.'

'Where is this?'

'Brazil.'

'Brazil? Not too far from here.'

She close the book. I add, 'You're lucky to have your mother. Mine never even leave behind anything for me.'

'You wish she did?'

'Yeah.'

'What was she like?'

'She die before I could remember her.'

She avert her eyes, bundling up the blanket between her fingers. She didn't say anything. I offer her some water, but she refuse it.

I tell her, 'There ain't much I could do bout it. Had to move on with my life. I understand you's a smart girl. Me, I ain't so smart sometimes.'

She purse her lips. 'Smart has nothing to do with it.'

'Smart can get you anywhere you want. Smart can save you a whole lotta trouble. You want to travel?'

'When my mom comes back, we're going to travel.'

I point to the scrapbook. 'She say that in the letters?'

'She doesn't have to.'

I give her a smile. 'Sounds excitin.' Then I add, 'Had this book I read when I was a boy. *The Little Prince*. Heard of it?'

She shake her head.

'Bout this boy, hopping from planet to planet. There's this scene in the beginning of the book. The narrator – not the Little Prince – is a pilot, and he crashes his plane in the Sahara. Don't worry. He survives. He looks up and sees a young, blonde child. Sophisticated, like you.'

A smile break on her face and she let out a tiny snort.

I continue, 'Was a boy, though. The Little Prince. Fearless, though he was in this big desert.'

'How did he end up there?'

'Told you, he hops across planets. He just happen to be there at the time of the crash. I had this image in my mind long time, since I was a wee child. Since the first time I read it. This fearless child in this unknown planet – which comfort the narrator in a strange way. I use to think I coulda be that fearless child, hoppin from planet to planet. And I was for a while.' My mind flash back to Sanskrit – the way he take my hand and lead me into his shack. 'But I'm the narrator now. Crash-land back here in St. Asteria. With all these fearless children lookin up at me.'

She furrow her brow. 'I'm not fearless.'

'You will be.'

She just nod.

'One day, he come cross this man on his own planet. A

lamplighter. The lamplighter has to spend every minute lightin and puttin out the lamp.'

'Why?'

'Cause the planet is so small. A sunset happens every minute.'

'He's the only one on the planet?'

'Yes, yet he still does his job.'

'Who is he doing it for?'

'Himself, though he doesn't know it.'

She frown. 'That don't make sense.'

'It ain't make a lick of sense to me for a long time,' I say. 'Maybe he's afraid of the dark. You know one way to get rid of your fear?'

'What?'

'Face it,' I tell her. 'Maybe it ain't so bad. And I'm thinkin, maybe he should go one night without puttin on the lamp. See if the darkness ain't so bad… You ever wonder if your mother won't come back?'

She remain quiet.

'You ever have that fear?'

'She's busy lately.'

'I'm not sure.'

'Does your mother know?'

She remain quiet.

'You never talk to her bout your fears?'

She swallow hard.

'Or you're waitin to do that when she come back?'

'I can't –'

'I contacted her the other day. I can get her on the phone for you.'

'Contact, how…?'

'I think you should talk to her.'

'She's not in Trinidad.'

'I know. She's in New York.'

'But how did…'

'We can do this today. What better time than now?'

I bring the cordless phone into the room. 'Just gimme the nod and I can do it for you.' Sal's mother's name was Satha Javed. Learn that from her blog. Satha been living in New York for six months. Finally grounded, it seem, since she get married. Prob-

164

ably why she ain't write her daughter in a year. I come across an art portfolio she had online – mostly landscapes of Trinidad. From charcoal sketches of vantage points on Laventille to a grand oil painting of the colossal Hanuman murti in Carapichaima. But what really interest me lie within the click of a button in the bottom right of the site. Two words: *Contact Me*.

And so I did – under the guise of commissioning some work from her. She was reluctant to give me her number at first. But she was a starving artist, desperate to make ties with her native land. This was a week before. I had the number in my mind, fixed for this moment.

So, I tell Sal, 'You need to be fearless now.'

She was breathin hard. Her eyes wide-wide.

'Ready?'

She responded with the tiniest of nods. I put it on speaker phone and dial the number – the phone bill was gon be a killer.

The phone ring once.

Ring twice.

Then it pick up. The voice, scratchy at first, 'Satha Javed speaking.' The Trini dialect wash right out – coulda swear this freshwater Yankee grow up next door to the Empire State Building.

Sal's chest was heavin.

'Mrs. Javed,' I say, trying to drop my accent as well. 'Jordon Sant here.'

'Ah, yes, about the commission? You're calling from Trinidad?'

'Yes, yes. Though it's not me you should be dealing with.'

'Oh? So it's not for you?'

'I just contacted you on behalf of a friend. Her name is Saleema.'

Sal close her eyes, still breathin hard. She look like she woulda start hyperventilatin. A streak of doubt fly by me. Was this the best thing? I then say, 'Saleema Javed is her name. You two related?'

There was a long pause at the other end. Then a mumble, 'Repeat that, please?'

'Saleema Javed is the one you need to be speaking to.'

Long pause again. 'No. No relation.'

Sal suddenly whimper out, 'Mom?' She was on all fours on the bed.

'Is this a *sick joke?*' The connection crackled.

'No, ma'am. That will be you.'

'*Pardon me?*'

'You're the sick joke, ma'am.'

'*Don't fuckin call me ma'am!*'

Then the cut-off tone. I click the phone off. I did expect Sal to burst into tears, but she didn't. She kneel on the bed, her gaze glue to the mirror, a flitting, distant look in her eyes.

'She's not comin back,' I tell her. I'd rested *The Little Prince* on the counter, the copy I sprung from the library. I went to get it and I put it on the bed. 'Read it and tell me what you think.'

I was hoping she woulda see the message I wrote on the inside of the cover: *Grown-ups never understand anything by themselves, and it is tiresome for children to be always and forever explaining things to them.*

A quote lifted right from the first few pages of the book, but I still put it there.

She didn't look at *The Little Prince.* She pick up her scrapbook instead. She begin to slowly tear through the pages, her mouth twistin as she did, her cheeks scrunched up. She wipe her eyes, as she shred her mother's face in half.

'You know what we could do with that book?' I say, 'But we have to do it *now*, before Father and Ti-Marie get home.'

So, we lit a fire at the back of the parish – where Kitty used to have her Joyfires. I let Sal help out. I kick the foliage together and she line the stones round them. She set the scrapbook in the middle. I strike the match and she flick it right in. Bulls-eye. The whole thing went up in flames, her mother's resin-coated face warping as each photo singe and curl, a coil of smoke whipping in the midday breeze. The fire danced in Sal's eyes, her clammy cheeks slowly reddening to a hot flush.

I tell her, 'Hard part is over. The rest is a long road with no turning. When I was a child, we use to worry all the time – that nobody woulda be there to protect us. Not like how a mother and father would. But now, well, I ain't think it matter so much. Had somethin someone tell me when I was small. If you ain't got

166

nothin, and I ain't got nothin, then we ain't got nothin to give each other but ourselves – and that's somethin people hardly get in this world.'

She turn her eyes away from the fire to look at me, her face like stone. She ain't say anythin. We let the book burn for bout ten minutes. Then we sweep the ash into a black garbage bag and I tie a double knot in it. I hose the rest of the ash down into the runnel.

I knew I had done the right thing when dinnertime came. As all of us settle down at the big dining room table, Sal come creeping into the room. Ti-Marie didn't say nothin. She just tip her chin at one of the boys, who promptly get up to fetch Sal a fork and plate. She pull up a chair and ate with us. She didn't speak much. She had *The Little Prince* with her. She read while she ate.

Right in the middle of dinner, the power cut out.

The children scream, but Ti-Marie calm them down quick. We got the candles from the kitchen and we all finish our meal. It was… heartwarming. I don't know how else to describe it. Seeing these faces against the glow of the candle flames. Seein Ti-Marie – each curve, each sink of her features pronounced by their flare. Seein her like that make my heart feel warm. Somethin I ain't ever feel for anybody else. Not even Mouse. My fondness for Mouse feel more like an itch. I was glad to have it purge from my body.

Perhaps I was too young to know how to love.

The children help clear the table and we help them wash the dishes. We put candles in each room as we put them to bed. A lone dog howl in the distance. Another howl a reply to it. I look out the window. The world was shroud in darkness. There was only shapes, shaded in ink. No detail, except in the starlight. No clouds among them. Nothing between down here and space. Just a black sky going up forever towards God.

Ti-Marie and I went upstairs, candles in hand. We set them on the dresser and we kneel before the bed, and pray to God together. In the candlelight, you can't see much in the room, just gold outlines. In the formless figures the light couldn't touch, my past flash before me. I coulda see everything. The pages of *The Little Prince* scattered, flying through the rain. Sanskrit's last look of horror before the bullet bite him. Kitty's face as she realized her life would never be the same. Shari's twitchin body as the venom take hold of her veins. The American in the hotel. That man bleeding to death in the clinic.

All behind me now. All pushin me forward.

I have my sins, but they is just one side of me. Hopefully, a small side. God is watching over me, and I must do my best to pull these children up from the mire. It isn't just a task. It is a necessity. It is the way of the world. Somethin to live for. Somethin I could affix my existence to. A currency for my tithes, to repay my debts. To heal my wounds.

So there it is, my statement and testimony.

After we finish pray, Ti-Marie lock the door. A half minute later, her nightie and my pants was toss in a tangle on the floor. I crawl on top of her and looked at her face one last time before I lean over to blow out the candles. Before my breath touch the flame, I say, 'I'm in heaven.'

As the flame went out, our smiles dissolved into the darkness.

Kevin Jared Hosein currently resides in Trinidad and Tobago and is the Caribbean regional winner of the 2015 Commonwealth Short Story Prize. His first book, *Littletown Secrets*, was published in 2013. In addition to having fiction published in the Hugo Award-winning *Lightspeed* magazine and *Moko* (Caribbean Arts and Letters), his work has been featured in anthologies such as *Pepperpot, New Worlds, Old Ways: Speculative Tales from the Caribbean, Jewels of the Caribbean* and the Akashic Books series, *Mondays are Murder* and *Duppy Thursdays*. He has also been shortlisted twice for the Small Axe Prize for Prose. His poem, "The Wait is So, So Long", was adapted into a short film that was awarded a Gold Key in the Scholastic Art & Writing Awards.

RECENT CONTEMPORARY FICTION FROM TRINIDAD

Rhoda Bharath
The Ten Days Executive and Other Stories
ISBN: 9781845232931; pp. 180; pub. 2015; price £8.99

Rhoda Bharath's stories bring a very contemporary Trinidad of the internet and social media into an urgent but complex focus. Told through a distinctive range of individual voices, they visit the domestic and public spaces of a country moving too fast between the knowing innocence of its past and the experience of a globalised present where the words "shipping and transportation" have quite a different meaning in the thesaurus of the street corner.

Caught in the antagonisms of race, class and gender; schools that have become a battleground; the violence that comes with the trade in cocaine; and an Anancy politics where government power is the means to personal wealth made secure by favours to one's ethnic supporters, Bharath's characters are often engaged in a struggle to balance a desire for meaning and self-worth with the temptations of survival by any means.

What Bharath brings to these narratives is an elliptical economy of suggestion that invites the reader to make connections; a bold, prophetic voice of alarm over a world that seems to have lost its moral compass; and subtly empathetic insights into the inner lives of her vividly drawn characters, but also a witty eye for the absurdity of their pretensions.

Rhoda Bharath was born and lives in Trinidad. A writer, lecturer and blogger, she teaches at the University of the West Indies, St Augustine.

These and over 350 other Caribbean and Black British titles are available online from peepaltreepress.com; by mail order from 17 Kings Avenue, Leeds LS6 1QS, UK; or by phone on +44 113 245 1703.